CAUSATION

FIRST CHRONICLES OF JAMES

CAUSATION

FIRST CHRONICLES OF JAMES

James F. Causey

Lagrange Georgia

Causation
First Chronicles of James

iSeebookz Publishing Suite 300
Commerce Ave Suite 137B
Lagrange Georgia 30241.

Thank you for your support.

ISBN: 978-1-7347762-7-0
First Edition

Printed in the United States of America
10 9 8 7 6 5 4 3 2 1

Editors Yolanda Rowland & Emily Salisbury
Front Cover image: ©Sergey Nivens/ Adobe Stock
Cover designer Pink Studio LLC in collaboration with iSeebookz Publishing LLC

In dedication to my daughter Kayla
and
My late daughter Brandy

ACKNOWLEDGEMENTS

My sincere appreciation goes to all who helped in this journey. My son James and his wife Brittany, Ms. Jami Brown, and Dr. David M. Hall. Thank you all.

CONTENTS

THE VOID

CHAPTER 1

It was early morning when Bobbo stepped out of his house. The wind blew the hat off of his bald head as he walked down the street toward his friend, Frederick Spink's house. His hat traveled in the same direction; Bobbo knew sooner or later he'd catch up to it.

His given name was Bobby Bishop. He had lost a bet while in high school and had to shave his head. The girls all said he looked cute, so Bobbo decided to keep it this way. His mother said his head looked like a fishing bobber. His father called him Bobbo, and the nickname had stuck with him from that day on.

Frederick stood in his front yard, watching Bobbo run back and forth across the street. At first, he was a little confused; then shortly, he realized Bobbo was chasing his hat.

Frederick laughed as he stepped out onto the street. Frederick reached down and caught Bobbo's hat before it passed by him. Bobbo thanked his friend before putting it back on his head.

"Did you see the light show last night?" Bobbo asked.

"No, but my dad did. He said it looked like all the stars in Heaven were falling to the earth," Frederick replied.

"Yeah, something like that, and I believe some. "I believe a few of them made it," Bobbo said.

"Made it where?" Frederick asked.

"To the ground," Bobbo said, pointing vaguely to the ground. Frederick looked down at where Bobbo had pointed. Bobbo laughed. "I don't mean right there, but I swear some of them fell into the gully down by the river." Frederick followed Bobbo to the edge of the gully; he had never been afraid of anything in his life. However, the site of the object below struck fear in his mind.

"What do you think it is?" Frederick asked.

Bobbo looked at his friend. "I have no idea what it is, but if you want to know what I think, I think we should get the hell out of here," he said.

I'm going down there and take a closer look," Frederick said, ignoring Bobbo's aversion.

Bobbo grabbed Frederick's arm, looking dead into his eyes; Bobbo instructed, "You do know I'm not going down there with you." Frederick nodded his head, then started looking for a way down into the big gully.

Bobbo stood looking over the ledge. After some time, he saw Frederick walking along the bottom of the gully. "What are they?" he yelled.

"I don't know? It looks like some kind of capsule. It's safe, Bobbo. Come down here and help me turn it over." Frederick yelled up to him.

"How do I get down there?" Bobbo asked.

"Go down and follow the river. You will see where the gully starts," Frederick yelled. By the time Bobbo reached the capsule, Frederick had it standing on its end.

"Wow, it looks like a coffin. You know, if coffins were round," Bobbo said, staring at the foreign circular objects.

"So, you think these things fell from outer space?" Frederick asked.

Bobbo looked around. "I don't know where they came from, but from what I saw last night, there should be more of them...I only see these two?" he said, wondering out loud.

"There could be further up the gully," Frederick responded to his inquiry.

"I don't think so. If there was, we should have seen them from up top. What are we going to do with them?" Bobbo asked.

Frederick scratched the top of his head. He looked from one capsule to the other. "They're not that heavy. We can carry them down to the river. I'll run and get my father's truck, and we can put them in the barn behind your house," he said.

"Then what?"

Frederick shook his head. "I don't know, Bobbo. Let's just get them to the barn first, and then we can figure out what to do with them from there."

***

"What the hell do you mean 'you lost them'? How could you have lost them? All you had to do was watch the damn monitor!" Teye yelled.

Peye looked at her brother. "Don't you yell at me! I was watching the damn monitor. They were miles away from the earth's orbit. I had to pee, and then I went to get something to eat. When I came back, the screen was blank," she said.

"Play it back for me," Teye said.

"Okay, but I've already played it back several times. Watch this. There they are coming in this direction and then, here..."

Peye put her finger on the screen. "Nothing. Poof, they're gone," she said.

Peye tapped several keys on her computer. A map of Alabama appeared.

"I have mapped out the coordinates. From what I have learned, we are in a country called the "United States". You and I are in the state of "Washington". Their pods came down in this state. We are twenty-five hundred miles from Alabama."

"We have to go there," Teye said.

Peye held up her hand. "I already made the arrangements. We leave tonight. Our plane lands in the city of Birmingham. I will rent a car and drive us to where they are," she said.

***

Bobbo watched as Frederick backed the truck up next to the barn door. He didn't know what his friend had in mind. For some reason, Bobbo couldn't shake the uneasy feeling in his gut. "What are we going to do now?" he asked. Frederick didn't answer Bobbo's question. The only things on his mind were the capsules.

Once the capsules were unloaded, Frederick looked them over. There seemed to be some kind of latch, or maybe it was a lock. He had never seen anything like it.

"Have you ever picked a lock, Bobbo?" Bobbo sighed and looked up at the ceiling.

"What's wrong with you?" Frederick asked.

"What is wrong with me? No, the question is, what's wrong with you? I have been talking to you for the past fifteen minutes, and you haven't heard a word I've said, Frederick!" Bobbo yelled.

Frederick walked over and placed his hands on Bobbo's shoulders. "Look, Bobbo, I'm sorry. But, think about this… we could be on to something big. Hell, we could even become famous," he said.

"No," Bobbo said.

"No, what?" Frederick asked.

"No, I have never picked a lock, but my father has a cutting torch out back," he said.

Frederick shook his head from side to side. "No, no. We can't cut them. If we did, we might damage whatever is inside."

Bobbo walked over and studied one of the capsules and noticed a small dust-covered plate with writing on it.

"Hey, look here. I think I've found something. Have you ever seen this type of writing?" Bobbo asked Frederick.

Using the tail of his shirt, Frederick wiped the dust away. "I think it's Hebrew. I have a book in my study. Wait here, and I'll go get it," he said.

A few minutes after Frederick had left the barn, Bobbo heard what sounded like air hissing out of a car tire. Not wanting to turn around, he soon realized the sound was coming from the capsules. Running toward the entrance, Bobbo almost stumbled before the barn door, and his hands outstretched balanced him. He opened the door handle, yanked it open, and yelled for Frederick, but it was too late; the truck was gone. Bobbo slowly turned around as the hissing sound stopped. He felt a sinking feeling in the pit of his stomach. Bobbo instinctively knew the capsules were open. A man stood beside one of them, and a woman lay inside the other. They were both naked. Bobbo's first thought was to run, but he couldn't will his legs to move. He almost passed out from fright when the man...

***

Peye parked the rental car in front of an old store. The sign above the door read "Cherry's Grocery." An old woman had just stuck a key into a lock on the door. Peye waited until the woman had gone inside the store and then gave her a few minutes to get situated. She looked back at her brother as she stepped out of the car. He lay asleep on the back seat. She gently closed the door.

When she walked into the store, a strange fear came over her. She hadn't felt this way in a long time. The old woman stood up from behind the counter. She walked around and put her arm around Peye's shoulder.

"Why, look at you. Ain't you a pretty thing? You not from around here, are you? Of course not. I mean, look at you. Where you from, girl?" she asked.

Peye stepped back from the old woman. At this time, Teye came through the door. Before Peye could say anything, Teye shot the old woman in the head.

"Why did you kill her?" Peye yelled.

"She was holding on to you. I thought you were in danger."

Teye looked around. "Come on, help me put her in the trunk of the car," he said.

"No, leave her. Grab some food and let's get out of here," Peye said.

Peye pulled the car back onto the highway. As much as she wanted to chastise her brother, she couldn't. She knew Teye was protecting her when he killed the woman. They were not in the same world they had left behind over five thousand years ago.

They were in search of their parents. All of the pods were supposed to have been released from the ship at the same point in time. For some reason unknown to them, Peye and her brother had released a month earlier. Every pod had a tracking device. Peye's mother had given her a code in case of separation. It was she who had spotted the blinking red light on her monitor. It was also she who had lost track of them.

Peye pulled the car into the parking lot of a Super G Mart store. "Why are we stopping here?" Teye asked.

"Because we need a map. If I am right, their pods came down along a river near here," Peye said.

"What do you mean if you are right?" Teye asked.

"When I was tracking their coordinates, I needed one more number," Peye shrugged her shoulders. "I took a guess," she said.

Teye slammed his fist down on the dash of the car. "Let me get this straight... You are telling me we have traveled almost three thousand miles across this country on a 'guess'!" he yelled.

Peye reached across the seat and slapped Teye's face. "I'm not going to tell you again, Teye; stop yelling at me. And, yes, but let me ask you this question: Have I ever been wrong?" she said.

Teye hung his head. "Look, I'm sorry I yelled at you. It's just... well, I miss them," he said.

Peye reached over and touched her brother's hand. "Me too," she said.

***

Bobbo watched the naked man walk across the floor of the barn. The woman hadn't moved. The man reached inside the capsule and picked her up. Bobbo saw the man's legs buckle under her weight. Not knowing where his courage came from or why he did what he did, Bobbo ran over and took the woman from the man's arms.

Two horse blankets lay across the rail of one of the stalls. The man pulled them down and lay them on top of some hay. "Lay her down," he said in English. Bobbo did as he was asked, then stepped away. It wasn't until that moment that Bobbo realized he was looking at a naked woman. He wanted to turn his head out of respect but couldn't take his eyes off of her.

The man knelt beside her. He lifted her head then blew into her mouth. A minute later, the woman sat up. The man reached inside one of the capsules and brought out what looked to Bobbo like a large white bed sheet. He wrapped it around the woman, then tied it around her waist. He then wrapped another one around himself. Next, he reached back inside the capsule and brought out what Bobbo assumed to be a cell phone. He punched in several numbers, stared at the screen for a moment, then showed it to the woman. She said something, but in a language, Bobbo didn't understand.

Bobbo looked up as Frederick entered the barn; within a second, the man had traveled the length of the barn, grabbed Frederick by his shirt, and shoved him against the wall. Neither Bobbo nor Frederick had ever seen anyone move this fast.

"Wait! He's, my friend!" Bobbo yelled. The man released Frederick and, within a second, stood beside the woman. Bobbo ran over to Frederick. "Are you alright?" he asked.

"Yeah, sure. I'm okay. How did you get the capsules opened?" Frederick asked.

"They just opened by themselves, and you are not going to believe this. They were both naked." Bobbo pointed toward the horse blankets. "I carried the woman, naked, to those blankets. Then the man gave her CPR, and she came alive. Then he wrapped them both in those sheets," he said.

Bobbo stopped speaking as he was still reeling over all that had happened.

Frederick walked to within a few feet of the man. "Who are you? And where did you come from?" he asked.

The man looked at the woman, then nodded his head. It was she who spoke, this time in English.

"We had already decided to kill you both, and you must understand that it is still a possibility, but right now, we need your help. It is not important who we are or where we came from. What is important is our two children. They are on their way to this place, but we are not certain that they know our exact location. One of you must guide them. You must also know this; if you fail, we will kill the other," she said.

Frederick reached for the man. Before he knew what had happened, he lay flat on his back, looking up at the man who held a strange-looking knife at Frederick's throat. The woman walked over and looked down at him. "You must never underestimate us," she said. Frederick realized that he had done precisely what she'd said not to. He had sized them up in his mind, the woman five foot three, weighing no more than one hundred pounds. She had long black hair, blue eyes, and her skin looked like she had been out in the sun or inside a tanning bed. The man was a few inches taller and outweighed the woman by twenty pounds. He, too, had long black hair and tanned skin. Frederick knew he outweighed the man by at least forty pounds and should have been able to take him down but had underestimated the man's speed.

Once again, Bobbo found himself pleading for the life of his friend. "Please, don't hurt him. We will do whatever you ask. We don't know where you came from or how you got here. Last night, there were many lights in the sky, and this morning we found whatever those things you came out of down by the river. We brought you here, but we didn't know it was you. I mean, we thought they were just some kind of capsules. We didn't know you were inside them." Bobbo knew he was babbling, but he didn't want whoever these people were to hurt Frederick.

The woman looked at Bobbo. "All we want you to do is help us find our children, and I give you my word you will not be harmed."

"We will do whatever you ask," Bobbo said.

Bobbo and Frederick listened to the man and woman hold a conversation in a language neither of them could understand. Then the woman spoke to them in English, "We think it is time to end your confusion on who we are and how we ended up down by your river. Would you like to sit?" she asked.

Bobbo sat down on a bale of hay, and Frederick stood beside him. "I had rather stand," he said.

"As you wish. My name is Gnay, and this is my husband, Mahog. We come from a place called the Void, but we were born on this planet over five thousand years ago. During that time, a great plague came, killing everyone in its path. So, the gods of the Void came down and brought with them a giant airship. Inside their ship were thousands of those pods, and we were placed inside them. Once they were closed, our conscience took over our minds. Although we were unconscious inside the pods, we believed we were living on another planet, a planet much like this one, only we never grew old, and there was no death among our people.

Several months ago, something happened. We know not what. Our pods were opened, and we were told by the gods we were being sent back to our own planet. When we asked about the plague, we were informed that the plaque didn't kill everyone, and the people who now lived on our planet would not understand. They would be afraid of us and would kill us on sight. We were told it would be better for us if we killed you, people, first." The woman walked over and touched Bobbo on the top of his bald head. She looked down at him. "Mahog said when our pods opened, he was weak. He said I was not breathing, and this one ran to his aid. It is with regret I know I may have to kill him. I told you we would not harm you if you helped us find our children, but there is more for you to understand. You must not tell anyone we exist until after we have departed," she said.

"Just tell us what it is you want us to do," Frederick said. Mahog spoke up.

"We were supposed to dock in our homeland." He reached inside the capsule and brought out another handheld monitor. "According to this, we are several thousand miles from our land. All we want to do is find our children and go home." He handed the monitor to Frederick then pointed to the two blinking red lights on the screen. "This tells us our son, Teye, and our daughter, Peye, are alive. What is the name of this land?" he asked.

"We are in Alabama," Frederick said. Mahog reached over Frederick's shoulder and punched in another code. An outline of the state appeared on the screen. Frederick studied the screen for a moment, then looked at Mahog. "According to this, your children are in the city of Wetumpka," Frederick placed his finger on the screen, then slid it down. "We are here, but there is a small problem," he said.

Gnay walked up beside them. "What is the problem?" she asked.

"Your children are traveling in the wrong direction," Frederick said. He saw the expression on Mahog's face change. He reached over and touched his arm. "Look, mister, you can do one of two things. You can trust us, or you can kill us. If you let me, I will find them and bring them here." Frederick waited a moment for this to sink in. Mahog looked at Gnay and then nodded his head. "Three things: I must go alone, I will need to carry this monitor, And I must leave now," Frederick said.

"How are you going to find them?" Mahog asked.

"Come," he gestured. "Follow me outside, and I will show you," Frederick said. Once they were all outside, Frederick pointed toward his father's pickup truck. "This is my means of transportation. It travels fast, but as I said, I need to leave now," he said.

"Wait one second," Gnay said. A second was all she needed to go back inside the barn, retrieve a photograph, and then returned to Frederick's side. "These are our children," she said. Frederick looked at the picture and then put it inside his shirt. He looked over at his friend. Bobbo nodded his head.

***

Jack and Jessie Adams sat in the swing on the porch of their farmhouse. "Would you look at that?" Jessie said, pointing her finger toward the sky.

"Well, I'll be damned. If I didn't know better, I would say God just set off a whole bunch of fireworks," Jack said.

"Looks to me like a whole bunch of shooting stars, except they are coming right at us," Jessie said. She stood up, walked down the porch steps, and out into the yard. She turned her head in time to see something crash through the roof of one of their chicken houses. The ground beneath her feet shook as something else plowed into the yard at the side of their house. Jessie screamed.

Jack jumped off the porch and grabbed her hand. "Get back inside the house," he yelled.

Instead of going toward the house, Jessie pulled Jack over to one of the big oak trees in their front yard. "It's safer out here. Look at the chicken house!" she yelled.

Jack and Jessie stood under the oak tree for a half-hour after the lights stopped falling. They heard the truck coming down the dirt road. They didn't have to turn around to know it was their son, Tony. He and his wife, Cathy, lived a quarter-mile down the road.

Tony slid his truck to a stop in front of the house. Jack and Jessie walked out to meet him. "Are y'all alright?" he asked.

"Yeah, we're okay. Where is Cathy?" Jack asked.

"She went to check on her grandmother. What were all those damn lights?" Tony asked.

"I don't know, but we can find out. One of them fell inside the chicken house, and there is another one around on the side yard," Jack said.

"Well, it ain't no meteor," Tony said as they looked down into the hole.

"What do you think it is?" Jessie asked.

"Could be a part of one of them satellite things they put out in space," Jack said.

Jessie walked over to the chicken house. When she opened the door, she had to jump aside as several chickens ran past her. "There is another one of those things in here!" she yelled.

Jack ran into the house. A few minutes later, he walked back outside. "I tried the phone. It's dead. Jessie, why don't you turn on the TV and see if you hear any news about those lights? Tony and I will see if we can get this one out of that hole," he said.

Thirty minutes later, Jessie came out of the house. Jack and Tony had both of the strange-looking objects laid out on the ground beside Tony's truck. "There ain't nothing on the news. What are y'all going to do with those things?" Jessie asked.

"We are going to take them to town and show them to the Sheriff," Jack said.

The hissing sound caused the three of them to jump back away from the objects. The first one, then the other, slowly opened. "Well, I'll be damned. Would you look at that?" Jack said.

"I knew they were some kind of space capsules," Tony said.

"Yeah, but who could have imagined something like this?" Jessie asked.

A naked woman lay inside one of the capsules. Jessie placed her hand on the woman's head. "Cold as ice. Been dead a while," she said.

"Looks like the man is dead, too," Jack said.

Tony opened the door on his truck. "I'll go to town and get the Sheriff," he said.

Two hours later, Sheriff Robert Tanner, four of his deputies, and Walter Evans, the county coroner, stood looking at the two dead bodies. "What do you think of this, Walter?" Sheriff Tanner asked.

"I don't know. Old Jack over there said they fell out of the sky during that light storm," Walter said.

Sheriff Tanner shook his head from side to side. "You know, Walter, you and I ain't never seen anything like this... but something tells me we need to keep an open mind on this one," he said.

"Yeah, I know. I read a while back where they had one of these light shows over in Egypt, but whatever fell over there blew holes in the ground the size of two football fields," Walter said.

Sheriff Tanner walked over to where the woman lay. He placed two fingers alongside her neck. "There ain't no pulse. I already checked," Walter said. More cars started arriving on the Adams' farm. Sheriff Tanner realized the man and woman still lay naked for all to see.

"For Christ's sake, Walter, get some sheets and cover those bodies," he said.

"I can go ahead and bag 'em if you want," Walter said.

"No, just cover them. I put in a call to the feds. They are on their way. Said they 'would be here around daybreak'," Sheriff Tanner replied.

It was four o'clock in the afternoon when Sheriff Tanner called the morgue. After several rings, a voice came on the line.

"Evans here. How can I help you?"

"Hey, Walter. I know you were up all night. I didn't wake you, did I?" he asked.

"Naw, the feds have been here all day working with those two bodies. What's on your mind, Sheriff?" Walter asked.

"Can you stop by my office on your way home? I have something I want you to see," Sheriff Tanner asked.

"Sure thing. I'll be there in a few minutes," Walter said.

Sheriff Tanner read the file that lay in front of him. Things like this weren't supposed to happen in his county. Lost in thought, he didn't hear the door to his office open. When he looked up, Walter stood in front of him. "I'm sorry, I didn't hear you come in. Have a seat, Walter," he said. He laid the file on top of his desk. "Did you hear about old lady Cherry? She was shot in the head with a .22 caliber handgun."

"Yeah, but that happened over in Elmore County. Their coroner is taking care of her," Walter said.

Sheriff Tanner opened the file, then spun it around for Walter to see. "I believe somehow all of this is connected. Cherry had a camera set up inside her store, and I saw the tape. On it was a young man and a woman, but it was the man who shot Cherry. And get this…the two on the tape looked eerily similar to those two dead bodies," Sheriff Tanner said.

"I still don't understand what it is you are trying to say here," Walter said.

The Sheriff leaned back in his chair. He looked up at the ceiling. "Remember me telling you, we would have to keep an open mind on this thing? Well, this was what I was talking about. Seeing those contraptions with the bodies inside, and considering they fell from the sky… Walter, don't you see? Those things are not from this planet, and there is no telling how many of them are out there," he said.

Walter stood up and placed both of his hands on the Sheriff's desk. He took another look at the folder. "Well, we do know for a fact that there are at least two of them. And we know they are alive. And we know they are killing people," he said.

One of the Sheriff's deputies walked into his office. "Hey, sheriff, sorry to bother you. Dispatch said they've spotted a man and woman fitting the description of the people who killed Ms. Cherry. Deputy Bone has all the details in her office," he said.

Deputy Susan Bone stood as the Sheriff walked into her office. She handed him a folder. "It's them, alright. Montgomery faxed us the photos from a cruiser camera. Sheriff, they killed two city police officers in cold blood. The man shot one of the officers, but, get this… the woman broke the other one's neck with her bare hands."

"Where are they now?" Sheriff Tanner asked. "They lost them, but they do have a statewide BOLO out on a blue Ford rental car," Susan said.

"Damn! Damn! Damn!" Sheriff Tanner said as he sat down on the edge of Susan's desk.

"It's bad, ain't it, Sheriff?" Susan said.

"Yeah, and I believe it's going to get a lot worse before it's over."

***

Frederick drove his father's truck down the Atlanta Highway in Montgomery, Alabama. He had never seen as many police cars at one time in his life, and he realized he had gotten into more than he had bargained. Pulling into the parking lot at Tink's Truck Stop, he needed three things, to use the restroom, to gas up the truck, and to get a strong cup of coffee to keep him going.

Two city police officers were talking to the girl behind the counter. Frederick sat in a booth close to them, hoping to hear why the police were out in such force. What he heard made him sick to his stomach. Two people, fitting Teye and Peye's description, had killed two cops. His mind went back to something Gnay had said. Because people now inhabiting the planet would be afraid, she said they were told to kill first.

Dismissing the thought, Frederick focused on his task at hand. He figured he would find Teye and Peye by using the monitor but wasn't sure how he would convince them that their parents had sent him.

He ordered a sandwich and another cup of coffee, this time to go. After paying, he hurried back to the truck. The blinking red lights on the monitor hadn't moved. If his calculations were correct, he should find Teye and Peye five miles south on Highway 231. He had forgotten about buying gas at the truck stop. He parked the truck alongside the highway where he believed Teye and Peye should be. According to the monitor, he should be right on top of them. Several cars slowed as they passed by. Frederick looked in both directions, making sure the road was clear, then did the only thing that came to mind.

He stepped out of the truck. "Teye! Peye!" he yelled. He walked toward a crop of pine trees beside the highway. He let a couple of cars go by, then shouted again. "I know you can hear me! Mahog and Gnay sent me!"

Teye came running from among the trees, and within seconds he had a gun against Frederick's head.

"Don't shoot. I am a friend. Your mother and father sent me to find you. They are waiting for you at my friend's house," he said. Frederick didn't see the young woman until she was standing in front of him.

"How do we know this is not a trick? I know my mother; she would have sent proof," she said.

Frederick reached into his shirt pocket, which made Teye pulled the hammer back on the gun. Frederick held up both hands. "Hold on, there. I'm just going to show you a picture," he said. Peye reached inside Frederick's shirt pocket and took out the picture. "I also have the monitor that led me to you," he said.

Peye put the picture back inside Frederick's pocket. "This proves nothing. You could be leading us into a trap," she said.

Frederick looked over at Teye. "You can kill me now if you want, but I promise, if you do, you will never see your parents again. There are over three hundred police officers between them and us. You have killed two of their own. Every one of those officers has blood in their eyes and will shoot you on sight. Now, what we need to do is get into that truck and off of this highway," he said.

After a brief pause, Teye grabbed his sister's hand. "He's right. Get into the truck," Teye said.

Frederick pulled the truck back onto the highway while Peye sat next to him; Teye sat next to the door.

"How long will it take for us to reach our parents?" Peye asked.

"A couple of hours. We will have to take the backroads around the city, but first, we will have to stop for gas." He pulled the truck into the parking lot of a church.

"Why are we stopping here?" Teye asked.

"There is a gas station up ahead. I am not risking the two of you being seen. I want you to wait here behind this church, and I will be back to pick you up in a few minutes."

Teye held up the .22 revolver. "Will you require this?"

"That's a pretty old gun. Where did you get it?" Frederick asked.

"From the old woman's car."

"What old woman?" Frederick held up his hand. "Never mind, I don't want to know. And, no, I won't need the gun. Get rid of it."

Frederick could feel his heart pounding inside his chest as he pulled up next to the gas pumps. Two police cars had been following him ever since he left the church. One of them drove past him and then backed up to the pump in front of the truck—the other police car parked behind him.

Frederick stepped out, removed the gas cap, then placed the pump nozzle inside the tank. He took his gas card out of his wallet. When he looked up, one of the officers was standing in front of him.

"You will need to go inside," he said.

"Excuse me?" Frederick said.

"To pay for the gas. These are old pumps. They don't take cards. You will need to go inside," the officer said.

"Oh, uh…. okay," Frederick turned toward the building. Before he had taken a step, he dropped his wallet. When he bent over to pick it up, the picture of Teye and Peye fell out of his shirt pocket. The officer reached down, picked up the image, looked at it, and handed it to Frederick.

"Friends of yours?" he asked.

"Uh… yeah," Frederick said.

After paying for the gas, Frederick walked back to the truck. Both officers stood beside the car in front of him, talking. He finished pumping his gas, got back into the truck, and started the engine. The officer realized that Frederick's exit was blocked by his car, so he pulled forward enough for Frederick to pass. Both officers threw up their hands and waved as he drove by.

Frederick drove a couple of miles past the church. He wanted to be sure the officers weren't following him. Fifteen minutes later, Peye sat next to him as he drove down the backroad around the city.

***

Sheriff Tanner walked out of the building. It had been a long day. He didn't expect it to get longer, but before he reached his car, his phone vibrated in his pocket. He flipped it open and saw that the call was from Susan. Instead of answering, he walked back to her office. She stood up, motioned for him to have a seat in the chair, and then handed him the phone.

"It's the Clanton police," she said.

The Sheriff listened for a few minutes, then covered the mouthpiece with his hand. "Call Roy and Oscar and tell them to meet me somewhere down Highway 31 toward Wadsworth," he said.

Susan left the room. A few minutes later, she walked back in. "Said they would meet you at the old skating rink." The Sheriff looked up and nodded his head.

***

Forty-six-year-old Oscar and forty-nine-year-old Roy Glenn were brothers. Roy joined the Autauga County police force right out of high school. Oscar did a two-year bid in the U.S. Army and then decided to join his brother as a police officer.

Oscar pulled his car into the parking lot of the old skating rink just north of Prattville. A few minutes later, Roy pulled up beside him. Oscar rolled down his window.

"What's going on?" he asked.

"All I know is that the Sheriff wanted us to meet him," Roy said.

"I think it has something to do with those people from outer space," Oscar said.

"Yeah, but I don't believe they are really from outer space. I think some idiots tried to launch a homemade rocket out of their backyard and got themselves killed in the process," Roy said.

"I don't know, Roy. When we were at the Adams' farm, I overheard the Sheriff and Walter talking, and I swear they think aliens are invading us," Oscar said.

"Well, we will know soon enough because here comes the Sheriff," Roy said.

The three of them stood in front of the Sheriff's car. Oscar and Roy watched as the Sheriff unfolded a map and spread it out on the hood.

"I know it's already been a long day, but it looks like it just got longer. The Clanton police got a call from a man who said he saw two young men hauling two of those capsules, or whatever they are, on the back of a truck. Said they put them in a barn behind the Bishop's place. The man said he's been watching them from the old cotton gin. The guy driving the truck left some time ago, but the other young man, along with a couple of people wrapped in white sheets, are still inside the barn," the Sheriff said.

"We don't need the map. I know where they are. We can drive over to the Varners' old place. We'll go through the backyards, walk down to the railroad tracks, and approach the gin from the back. No one will be able to see us coming," Oscar said.

The man who made the call met them on the second floor of the old cotton gin. He introduced himself as Allen Parker.

"Are they still inside the barn?" the Sheriff asked. Allen nodded his head.

"Yes, as far as I know. I haven't seen hide nor hair of them since the young man in the truck drove off."

Oscar walked over and looked out the window. The Sheriff walked up behind him. "What are you thinking?"

Oscar pointed toward the tracks. "I can go back up the tracks, then come in behind the barn."

"Sounds good. Roy and I will give you twenty minutes; then, we will go in through the front door," the Sheriff said.

Allen looked at Oscar. "I can go with you."

The Sheriff reached down and unclipped the radio from his belt. "No, you take this, and if any shooting starts or if you see anything go wrong, you call Susan. Tell her to send the state police to our location."

Oscar stood at the back of the barn. It had taken him longer than twenty minutes to reach it. He could see inside through a small crack in one of the siding boards. He had to cover his mouth with his hand to hold back his scream. Roy lay on the floor of the barn; blood covered his face. The Sheriff lay a few feet behind him. A man and woman stood next to their bodies. As soon as Oscar stepped through the opened back door, he shot the man in the back. The woman moved faster than anyone Oscar had ever seen as she ducked behind one of the capsules. Oscar fired twice more in her direction. The woman stood up as if daring Oscar to shoot her, but before he could pull the trigger, she vanished from his sight.

Oscar ran over to where his brother lay. He felt relief seeing Roy's chest moving up and down. Crawling over to the Sheriff, Oscar placed his two fingers along his neck. He pulled the radio from his belt. "Susan, Roy is hurt bad. I think the Sheriff is dead. Call everyone you know!" he yelled into it. Allen's voice came over the radio. "I've already called her. They're on their way," he said.

"Don't shoot. I'm coming out, and I ain't got no gun," Bobbo yelled.

Oscar jumped to his feet, pointing his gun in the direction of the voice. He watched as the young bald man stepped out from behind a stack of hay bales. "Who are you?" Oscar asked.

"My name is Bobby Bishop. I live here," he said.

Oscar took a few steps closer. "Okay, Mr. Bishop. Here is what I want you to do. First, turn around and get down on your knees. Then, I want you to put both hands on top of your head." Bobbo did as he was told. Oscar walked up behind him. "Now, put both hands behind your back," he said. Again, Bobbo complied with his request. Oscar took the handcuffs from his belt and put them on Bobbo. "I'm going to help you to your feet. Then, I want you to sit down on that bale of hay over there and tell me what the hell happened here," Oscar said.

"It's all our fault. They didn't have to kill nobody! I tried to stop them. It's all our fault," Bobbo cried.

Oscar heard the ambulance. His mind went back to his brother. "Don't you move!" he yelled at Bobbo. He took his handkerchief from his pocket and wiped some of the blood off of Roy's face. "Hold on, Roy. You're going to be okay. Help is on the way," he said.

Oscar helped load Roy into the ambulance, then walked back inside the barn. Bobbo stood beside one of the capsules. "I told you not to move!" Oscar yelled.

"I know, but listen to this thing... It's ticking loud," Bobbo said, not knowing they'd be his last words.

Twenty miles away, Frederick saw the fireball racing up into the sky. He felt the highway shake beneath the truck. He saw the three police cars blocking the road.

"Stop the truck!" Teye yelled, and Frederick slammed on the brakes and looked into the rearview mirror. He saw the two police cars from the gas station pull in behind them. Teye stepped out of the truck, raising his gun to shoot. The top of Teye's head exploded as fired shots came from the officers. Frederick heard the windshield crack and saw Peye fall from the truck. Realizing it was more than he bargained for, the truck's back window exploded, and Frederick heard no more.

****

Seven-year-old Cody Landcaster ran through the door of his house in Addison, Alabama. "Ma Ma, Daddy, the stars are falling out of the sky!" he yelled.

Jerry Landcaster looked up from the newspaper he was reading. "What's that boy yelling about?" he asked his wife, Shirley.

"Let me get this bread out of the oven, and I'll go see," she said.

"Ma, Ma!" Cody yelled again.

Shirley wiped her hands on her apron before stepping out the back door. The sky was lit up with what looked like shooting stars, just as her son stated. Some of them seemed to be falling to the ground. Cody pointed toward the open field next to their house. "I saw some of them fall out there," he said.

Shirley stuck her head back inside, calling for her husband.

Jerry came out of the house in time to see a few of the lights. "You should have seen it earlier. There were hundreds of them," Shirley said. Cody ran into the field. "Hey! You come back here this minute!" Shirley yelled.

"Where the heck is he going?" Jerry asked.

"He thinks some of whatever they were fell out in the field. Let me get a flashlight, and we'll go see what he's talking about," Shirley said.

Fifty yards out into the field, they found Cody standing beside a small space capsule. Shirley shined the flashlight around in a circle. "There are two of them," she said. Shirley handed Jerry the flashlight, then took her phone out of her jeans' pocket, dialing 911, but nothing happened. She hung up, then hit redial; still, nothing—the phone wasn't receiving a signal in the field.

"Let's go back to the house," she said. They had taken a few steps when they heard a hissing sound coming from the capsules. Jerry turned around, shining the flashlight on the capsule; the top halves of both had opened. A man and woman lay naked inside of them. Jerry shined the light on the woman as she jumped out of the capsule. Within seconds, she stood beside the man's capsule, and then it was like she had vanished into thin air. Another hissing sound came from further out in the field.

Jerry shined the light in its direction. "There is another one out there," he said.

The unfamiliar woman stood beside it. She reached inside the capsule and brought out a small child. Again, she vanished. Before Jerry had time to turn around, the woman stood beside them. She looked at Shirley. "Will you hold my daughter while I see to my husband?" she asked.

Jerry saw the woman trying to lift the man out of the capsule. He ran to her side. "Let me help," he said. He placed his hand on the man's chest, then reached down and picked him up. Jerry looked at the woman, "He's alive. I'll carry him over to our house."

"Get me a blanket," Jerry said as he lay the man down on the couch inside their home. He covered the man with the blanket Shirley had given him.

"How is he?" the woman asked.

"He seems to be breathing okay," Jerry said.

Shirley saw the baby move in the woman's arms. She looked down into a set of beautiful blue eyes. "How old is she?" she asked.

"She is two earth years," the woman said.

It wasn't until then that Shirley realized the woman was still naked. "Oh, God. I'm so sorry. Come with me. I'll find you some clothes." The woman looked down at the man. "Don't worry. He's in good hands. My husband is a medic in the Army."

"National Guard," Jerry said.

Shirley laughed. "Same thing," she said.

Shirley weighed one hundred and sixty pounds and stood five feet, nine inches tall. None of her clothes would even come close to fitting the woman. She took a pair of her son's underwear and one of her husband's oversized sweatshirts. She led the woman into the bathroom. The woman looked confused when Shirley turned on the shower. "It's for bathing," she said.

Shirley took the baby from the woman's arms and walked out of the bathroom. Once again, a realization came to her when she saw Cody standing in the hallway. He had not spoken a word since the whole ordeal started. "Are you okay, little man?" she asked him.

"Yeah, I'm alright," he said.

"Good, because I need you to watch her. Can you do that for me?"

"I can do it," Cody said as he crawled up onto his bed.

Shirley walked back to the living room. The man sat on the couch with a blanket wrapped around him. Jerry sat beside him. The man looked up at her. "Where are my wife and daughter?" he asked.

"Your daughter is asleep. My son is watching her. Your wife is getting cleaned up. She will join us in a few minutes." Shirley sat down on the edge of their coffee table, facing the man.

"My husband and I have remained calm through this whole ordeal. In my mind, I have tried to figure out where and why you people got into those capsules. When your wife didn't know what a shower was for, well, that kind of freaked me out. So will you please just tell us who you are and where the hell you came from?" Shirley asked.

The man stood up. "We should wait for my wife. She will explain everything to you. But first, I must return to our pods. We have other family members who came down with us. I have some equipment that will help us locate them," he said.

"Do you have clothes in your pod?" Shirley asked.

"Yes, but not like the clothes that you wear. We have our wraps."

Jerry stood up. "I'll go with you," he said.

"It will not be necessary. I assure you I am alright, and it will be faster if I go alone," the man said. Thirty seconds later, the man walked back inside the house, wrapped in a white cloth, holding a small computer monitor.

The four of them sat around the kitchen table. The man spoke in a language neither Jerry nor Shirley understood. Finally, the woman looked over at them. "What do you want to know about us?" she asked.

"For starters, how about your names?" Shirley said.

"Yes, of course. My name is Effect, and this is my husband, Jok. Our daughter's name is Lease."

"Okay. My name is Shirley, my husband's name is Jerry, and our son's name is Cody. Now we would like to know where you come from," Shirley said.

"Before I tell you, I ask that you keep an open mind, for this may be hard for you to believe."

"I assure you, tonight's events have already blown our minds, so nothing you might say will shock us," Shirley said.

"We were born on this planet five thousand earth years ago. At the time, our land had no name placed on it, but now we understand that you people call our land Egypt. Everyone in our land was dying. The gods sent a great airship, but the ship wasn't large enough for every family. Our men fought for the right to have their own family aboard. It was my father who fought for us. He was injured in the fight and died after we boarded the ship. Our family consists of the three of us, my sister, her husband, and their two children. We were locked inside our pods. In our minds, we were taken to a place called the Void, and there we lived until now."

"Let's say for now we believe you. You say you lived in the Void for five thousand years, a place where you obviously do not age. So, why come back here?" Shirley asked.

"Not long ago, the gods opened our pods. They did not tell us why but told us we were being sent back to earth. They gave each of us one of these monitors and said we were implanted with a chip that will allow us to know our family members' location. We had to learn several languages, how to use your weapons, and your current means of transportation. We were told about the violence on this planet, and we were supposed to kill everyone we came into contact with. Do you have more questions?" Effect asked.

"Yes, I definitely have more questions. You say you were supposed to kill us, yet you didn't. And if I understand you right, you seem to believe everyone on our planet is violent. I want you to know, and you must believe this, what you were told is not true. I am not saying that there aren't some bad people, because there are, but most people believe in doing good. Jerry and I didn't help you because we wanted something from you. We helped you because we know in our hearts it was the right thing to do," Shirley said.

Effect held up her hand. "I am sorry if I misled you. It's not as if Jok and I believe our lives are in immediate danger from the two of you. It's your government that will not believe we are from this planet. They will not believe we have lived the past five thousand years in the Void. They will try and locate all of our people and lock us away inside one of their prisons. We have... special abilities, so we will not allow this to take place."

"What kind of abilities?" Jerry asked.

Jok spoke up. "Our bodies have lived gravity-free for thousands of years. All of those years have given us the ability to travel at the speed of sound. We also have great strength. Where this comes from, we do not know."

Jerry's cell phone rang. He listened for a few moments, then looked at Shirley. "I'm going to take this outside," he said. When he walked back inside, Jok and Effect were looking at the monitor. He walked past them, went into his bedroom, and when he returned to the kitchen, he held his twelve-gauge shotgun in his hands.

"How far will they reach?" he asked.

"I do not understand your question," Jok said.

Jerry pumped a shell into the chamber. "I am asking about the blasts from your pods. I just got off the phone with my Sergeant. It seems some of your pods exploded in Wadsworth. It took out the whole town. Everyone is dead!" Jerry yelled.

Jok raised both hands above his head. "I assure you, Effect, and I mean you no harm. You and your wife have shown us great kindness, but the answer to your question is yes, our pods are equipped with an explosive device, but the only way they can be activated is with one of these monitors." Jok reached down and pushed the monitor across the table. "To prove my word is true, I'll give it to you," he said.

Shirley picked up the monitor and looked at the screen. She saw a single blinking red light. "What does this light mean?" she asked.

"It is what's left of our family," Effect said.

Shirley saw the tears running down Effect's face. "I don't understand," she said.

"Neither do we. The gods told us that our family would be released at the same point in time. There must have been some kind of mix-up. My sister's children were sent out in the first phase. Time passed, then my sister and her husband were sent out in the second phase. We were sent in the third phase. The light on the monitor means that besides the three of us, there is only one alive. The rest are dead," Effect said.

"Does this monitor tell you which one is alive?" Shirley asked.

"Yes, it is my sister. Her name is Gnay."

"Do you know where she is now?" Jerry asked.

"I will need to hold the monitor before answering your question," Jok said. Jok punched in a code. The state of Alabama appeared on the screen. He handed the monitor to Shirley. Jerry lay down the shotgun.

"Let me see it," he said.

"What do you think?" Shirley asked.

"From what I can see, she is in Birmingham, which is about sixty miles from here, and according to this light, she's moving this way fast," Jerry said.

Once again, Jerry's Phone rang. This time it was a text telling him to check his email. He walked back into his bedroom, opened his laptop, and reviewed the message. It was from his Sergeant. "PFC Landcaster: We are on our way to your home. If those people are still inside your home, kill them now! Your family is in grave danger!"

Jerry walked back into the kitchen, picked up his shotgun, and pointed it toward Jok. "I asked you a question that you have avoided answering, so I am going to ask you again." Jerry shifted the shotgun toward Effect. "I want you to understand, if you don't give me the correct answer, I will kill her," he said.

Jok nodded his head. "Ask your question. I will answer you," he said.

"The pods are set to explode. What is the range of the explosion?" Jerry asked.

"From the three pods, everything within fifty earth miles will be destroyed. The timer has already been set, and if you kill one of us, then your whole family will die," Jok said.

"I don't believe you!" Jerry yelled.

"Then this puts you in a real dilemma. You gamble with your family's life," Jok said.

Shirley picked up the monitor. "The light. It's not far away from us and moving fast," she said.

"May I see the monitor?" Effect asked. Shirley looked at Jerry, and he nodded his head. Effect studied the monitor. "She is running. She knows our location," she said.

"How long before she arrives?" Jerry asked.

Before Effect could answer Jerry's question, the front door flew from its hinges and landed on the living room floor. In the blink of an eye, the shotgun flew from Jerry's hands. He lay flat on his back, looking into Jok's eyes.

"I could have killed you one hundred times over. It was because of your kindness that I promised Effect I would not, but now it seems you and your wife have had a change of heart. When I told you the timer on our pods had been activated- that was true. Another truth is I alone can deactivate them. Your son sleeps in his bed. We have taken your wife. Effect, her sister, Lease, and your wife are already miles from here. Once I join them and see we were not followed, I will deactivate the pods and send your wife back. I give you my word," Jok said.

Jerry turned around. When he looked at the shattered front door, he saw a shadow cross his front porch. Jok never felt anything as the slug tore through his heart. Jerry looked at the soldier who stood in the doorway, holding his rifle. "You just killed us all," Jerry said.

***

Twenty-four hours later, Shirley opened her eyes. Her head hurt. She tried to reach up and touch it. It was then she realized her hands were tied to the arms of a chair. The only light came from a small TV set that sat in front of her. She didn't want to believe what was being said, then reality set in and tore a hole in her heart.

"Another explosion destroyed the small town of Addison, Alabama. As far as we know, there are no survivors. The FBI and Homeland

Security have the entire southeast blocked off. No one is allowed in or out at this time. It is believed that all people responsible for the explosions resemble these two. If you see anyone who looks like this, please call the number at the bottom of your screen." The picture of Peye and Teye appeared on the screen.

The overhead light came on. A woman walked down the basement steps. Although she looked exactly like Effect, Shirley knew it wasn't her. The woman stopped and stared at the TV screen. Tears ran down her face.

"Who were they?" Shirley asked.

The woman reached down and cut off the TV. "They were my children, and now they are dead. Everyone who came from the Void is dead. I am all alone now," she said.

"But what about Effect, Jok, and their daughter?" Shirley asked.

"Jok did not join us. Effect went back for him. I begged her to leave the child with me, but she refused. She thought it was more important for me to watch you. They, too, were killed in the explosion, so you and I have something in common."

It took a moment for Shirley to realize the truth in the woman's last statement. Jerry and Cody were also dead. Shirley dropped her head as tears uncontrolled fell down her face. She sat in shock, not wanting to believe her mind questioned a past thought.

Shirley was sure Effect had mentioned her sister's name, but for the life of her, she couldn't remember. "What is your name?" she asked.

The woman walked up the stairs, opened the door, then turned back and looked at Shirley. "It's Gnay," she said as she closed the door behind her.

Gnay returned, carrying a tray of food. Using a knife, she cut the ropes, freeing Shirley's hands.

"You must eat," she said.

"What are you going to do with me?" Shirley asked.

"If you fear for your life, then stop. I will not harm you," Gnay said.

Shirley reached down and picked up a glass of tea from the tray. She watched as Gnay studied the screen on one of the handheld monitors.

Gnay looked up at Shirley. "Do you know where I will find the River Nile?" she asked.

***

Zeedekin walked into the control room; his shipmate and lifelong partner was slumped over the control panel.

"Are you ill?" he asked.

"Only in my heart," Heenan replied. He stood up, shook his head, and looked back at Zeedekin.

"You, too, look ill," he said.

"How so?" Zeedekin asked.

"I can't put my finger on it, but you look different," Heenan said.

"Ah, we are no longer in the protection of the Void, so now we are in the aging process," Zeedekin said.

Heenan let out a laugh. "What do you mean? We are getting older?" he said.

"Yes, now tell me, my friend, how is your project going?" Zeedekin asked.

"Only one alive," Heenan said.

"One? We sent over a thousand pods to earth," Zeedekin said.

"Tell me something I don't know. We sent one thousand, two hundred and twenty-three, to be exact. Sixteen made it through. Fourteen have self-destructed, and as I said, one subject remains alive," Heenan said.

"Do you know the name of that one subject?" Zeedekin asked.

"This whole project has been one big screw-up, so if I am correct, the subject is a female who goes by the name Gnay," Heenan said.

"I do not remember her," Zeedekin said.

Heenan rolled his eyes toward the ceiling. "Of course, you don't," he said.

Heenan realized his mistake as soon as the words came out of his mouth. The last time he had offended his partner, Zeedekin had not spoken to him for over one hundred earth years.

"I dare you to mock me! This earth project was all your idea. My job was to help in releasing the pods. You were supposed to oversee them once they landed on earth. And, if you remember, it was I who told you that you were getting too attached to the subjects," Zeedekin yelled.

"Please forgive me, friend. You are correct on all accounts. Unfortunately, I cannot figure out where I went wrong, and I am sorry for my sarcasm," Heenan said.

"Do you plan to take our ship back to Earth and retrieve the one subject?" Zeedekin asked.

"No, that will not be necessary. I have sent Gnay a message instructing her to meet us on the bottom of the River Nile. I have set the coordinates; we are on our way back to the Void."

***

Three weeks later, Gnay stood naked atop a bridge. Egypt's River Nile rushed by below her. A crowd of people stood watching as she raised her hands above her head with one question for the gods of the Void. And in her mind, Gnay knew she would never know the answer.

"Why were we sent back?" she yelled before she jumped.

THE GIFT

CHAPTER 2

Sandy Easterling parked her old truck behind the house her mother had given her. She told the twins to go inside. She knew it was risky driving them to the hospital, but Carl had shown emotions she had never seen in her son. Sandy lay her head against the steering wheel. She knew that if people found out about her children, she would have to pack up and move once again, and life as they knew it would be over.

***

"Sarah!" Paul Wilkins yelled to his wife as his feet touched the floor. The bedside clock read ten a.m. He could hear the rain beating down on the tin roof of their cabin. His head felt like it was going to explode—results from the previous night's alcohol consumption. The birthday party had been for one of Sarah's friends who had turned thirty, and Paul has never been one to turn down a free drink.

Paul met Sarah while they were in high school. He was the captain of the football team. His coach told him he was failing his math class and would need to bring his grades up if he wanted to remain on the team. Sarah was considered one of the whiz kids, so Paul asked her to help him out. The two of them became friends but didn't start dating until Sarah's senior year in college.

Paul's father and his mother, Anna, owned a large cattle farm. Instead of college, Paul decided to stay at home and work for his parents. He spent most of his spare time by the lake on the backside of their land, working on his cabin.

One afternoon, while on his way home from town, Paul saw Sarah's car parked beside the road next to their property. Thinking she had broken down; Paul parked his truck behind her car. He saw her walking in the woods. He called out, asking if she was alright. Sarah came out of the woods. She told Paul she was looking for a Christmas tree. He was teasing her when he accused her of stealing a tree. She had a few choice words to say about his accusation, but Paul knew she was more embarrassed than angry.

That same afternoon, Paul cut down the best-looking tree on their land, loaded it on the back of his truck, then drove to Sarah's home. She accepted his apology, the tree, and his dinner invitation. Six months later, they were married and moved into the cabin.

"Sarah!" Paul yelled again as he came out of the bathroom. It wasn't until he walked into the kitchen that reality set in. Pieces of glass lay across the floor, and the window above the sink was broken. Paul's heart skipped a beat when he saw the blood. One large pool then drops leading out the door. He followed the drops across the porch and down the steps.

Beyond the steps, the blood had been washed away by the rain. Sarah's car was parked in its usual spot, but his truck was gone. He ran back through the cabin, looking for his phone. His jeans lay on the floor in their bedroom. He picked them up, searched the pockets, but the phone wasn't there. He slipped on his jeans and pulled a shirt over his head. He had just finished putting on his socks and boots when he heard his phone ring from somewhere inside the cabin. He ran to the living room. His phone lay on the floor beside the fireplace, but by the time Paul picked it up, it had stopped ringing.

Looking at the caller I.D, his father had called. He_hit the speed dial. Other than hello, he didn't give his father time to say anything else.

"Have you seen Sarah?" he asked.

"Yes, your mother has taken her to the hospital. Where the hell have you been?" his father yelled into the phone.

"I was in bed, asleep. What happened?" Paul asked.

"We don't know. Your mother found her inside your truck. It was parked in our yard when we got up. Paul, Sarah has been shot," his father said.

"I'm on my way," Paul said as he hung up the phone.

***

Twelve-year-old Carla Easterling watched as her twin brother, Carl, hide behind the big oak tree in their backyard. She knew he was up to something when she saw the baseball bat in his hands. But it wasn't until she saw their dog, Sam, walk around the corner of the house that she realized his intentions.

Since age six, Carl had amused himself watching her, not knowing he was her first recipient, using her gift. At age five, Carl had been bitten by a rattlesnake. Their mother carried Carl's dead body into the house. She instructed Carla to lay her hands on Carl's head, then 'to visualize him alive'. It was on their sixth birthday Carla made the mistake of letting Carl watch as she resurrected a cat that had been hit by a car. And it was on that same day Carl had killed their neighbor's dog so he could watch her 'do her thing,' as he called it.

"Carl, don't you dare!" Carla yelled.

Sam realized something was amiss, so he took refuge under the porch.

"Now, look at what you've done!" Carl yelled back at his sister. Carla walked over and grabbed Carl's arm.

"Listen to me, Carl. No more birds, no more dogs, or for that matter, any other animal. Do you understand me?" she yelled.

"Okay, okay. But there is one more thing I want you to do, but it's a good thing, I promise," Carl said. Carla stood, looking at her brother.

"Well?" she said.

"Well, what?" Carl replied.

"What is it you want me to do?" Carla asked.

"There is a buck deer over on the Wilkins's land. Its leg is hurt real bad. I see it every time I go over there. I thought maybe if I shot the deer, you could, you know, 'do your thing', and this deer's leg would also be healed," Carl said.

"I don't believe you. I think you just want to kill something," Carla said.

"No, I swear to you, Carla, the deer's leg is really hurt," Carl said.

"Okay, then, you go get your gun. If I see that the deer is hurt, then you can shoot it," Carla said.

"No, not now. We will need to wait until morning. The deer will be drinking water from the lake," Carl said. Early the next morning, Carla followed Carl across the field and around the lake. "There he is," Carl said. Carla watched as the deer hobbled back and forth along the water's edge. The deer stopped, raised its head, sniffing the air.

"I think he smells us," Carla said. A dark cloud moved overhead.

"No, he smells the rain." Just as Carl spoke, the rain came pouring down. The deer limped into the woods. "Come on. He won't go far," Carl said. The rain came down harder. Finally, the deer stood in a small clearing. Carla jumped when the gun went off beside her. The deer ran further into the woods.

"You missed it," Carla said.

The woman came out of the cabin. She had both hands pressed against her breast. She had blood dripping between her fingers.

"My God, Carl! You shot her!" Carla yelled. She took off, running toward the cabin. But, before she could make it, the woman got into the truck and drove away. Carla grabbed Carl's hand.

"Run, we have to go get mother. She will know what to do," she said.

***

Paul took Sarah's keys from the peg beside their back door. Twenty minutes later, he walked into the hospital. His mother, Anna, stood in the hallway, talking to one of the doctors. Tears ran down her face. No one had to say a word for Paul to know his wife was dead. He sat down in the first chair he saw. He couldn't hold back his tears. Anna walked over and put her arm around his shoulder.

Paul saw a nurse come running down the hall. She grabbed the doctor's arm, pulling him to the side.

"What!" the doctor yelled. The nurse stepped back.

"I just came from her room... she's alive," she said.

"That's not possible. The bullet was lodged inside her lung. She bled out... I pronounced her dead myself," the doctor said.

"What the hell is going on?" Paul asked.

"This has to be a mistake. Wait here; I'll go check it out," the doctor said.

"Like hell! We're going with you!" Anna said.

Sarah stood by the window, watching the twins walk across the parking lot. She turned around when Paul, Anna, and the doctor entered the room.

"Sarah, please, you must lie down. You've been shot," the doctor said.

"Don't be silly. I'm okay. We need to go home and get ready for Mary's party," Sarah said. Paul walked over and put his arm around her.

"Sarah, Mary's party, was yesterday. Don't you remember?" Paul took a deep breath, "Sometime this morning, you were standing inside our kitchen, and someone shot...." Paul stopped in mid-sentence. "Wait a minute- is this some kind of sick joke?" he asked.

Sarah looked at her husband, "No, no. I remember now. It was a little girl," Sarah said.

"What little girl?" Anna asked.

"They got into the old truck," Sarah said.

"They? Was someone with her?" Anna asked.

"Yes, a little boy. They were so young... and so cute," Sarah said.

***

Molly Taylor opened her eyes. The faint sound of her phone had awakened her. She looked at her bedside clock—three-thirty a.m. Who in the world could be calling her at this time of the morning, she thought? She crawled out of bed, fumbled through her purse, took out her phone, and answered it. The line was dead, but someone had left a message on her voicemail. "Molly, it's Larry. I've found Sandy and the twins. Call me." Molly punched in a number on her phone. "Dad, it's me. Larry found them," she said.

The following day as she drove up the mountain, Molly turned the dial on her radio.

The sound of bluegrass music took her mind back to their childhood. The whole family spent every Sunday at Maw Maw Mindy's house. Her sister, Ginger, their cousins, Sandy, and herself sang while her father and uncles played music. Those were considered the 'good old days', but it all ended the day Sandy's twins had been born. Until Carla, Molly's sister, Ginger, had been the last one in their family born with the gift of healing. When Molly's father had wanted to take the girl child and raise her as his own, Sandy took the twins and moved away. Until now, no one had been able to find them. From what Larry had told her, Carla's powers went far beyond the norm. She had raised a woman from the dead.

Molly saw Ginger sitting on the front porch when she pulled the car into the drive at Maw Maw Mindy's house. Before Molly got out of the car, Ginger opened the passenger door and slid in beside her. "Let's go for a ride. I have something I need to show you," she said.

"Okay, where to?" Molly asked.

"Go around the mountain to the Baker's farm," Ginger said.

Molly pulled the car back onto the highway, then turned down a dirt road that led them around the mountain. Neither of them spoke. They were almost to the Baker's farm when Ginger broke the silence.

"No one else has been born with the gift since Carla," she said.

"Do you still have the gift?" Molly asked.

"Yes, that's what I want to show you," Ginger said.

Molly pulled the car onto the Baker's property. "Drive all the way to the horse barn," Ginger said.

Once they were out of the car, Ginger led Molly to one of the stalls. Molly saw a mare standing next to her colt. Ginger placed her hand on

Molly's arm. "Mr. Baker called me three weeks ago. He said the mare was about to fold, but she was sick. He asked if I could come over and heal her. By the time I got here, the colt had come, and the mare was dead." Ginger didn't say anymore. She looked at her sister.

"Are you telling me what I think you're telling me?" Molly asked.

Ginger felt a chill go down her spine. She wondered if she had made a mistake telling Molly that she, too, could raise the dead. "Listen, Molly. We can't tell anyone, at least not for now," Ginger said.

"So, you, I, and the Bakers are the only ones who know?" Molly asked.

"No, no. The Bakers don't know. I told them their mare was asleep when I healed her, but there is one other person... Maw Maw Mindy died two weeks ago; I brought her back. She told me not to tell anyone. I told you because you and I have always been able to share everything, and I need your help," Ginger said.

"Let me guess…. Father?" Molly said. "Yes. He believes Carla is evil, and he plans to kill her," Ginger said.

"So, you want me to go back and warn Sandy," Molly said.

"Yes, and help her relocate. I'll go with you but right now, let's go back to Maw Maw's house before they realize I'm not there," Ginger said.

Maw Maw Mindy could tell by the way Molly looked at her that Ginger had revealed their secret. She reached out and put both hands on Molly's shoulders. "It's been a long time. How are you doing, child?" she said.

"I know I should have come to visit. I'm okay, but…." Maw Maw Mindy shook Molly's shoulders. "Hush, child. Listen to me. You and your sister go find that girl and keep her safe. Don't worry about your father, I'll take care of him. Do you understand what I'm telling you to do?" she asked. Molly nodded her head. "Good, now take your sister and go," Maw Maw Mindy said.

***

Doctor Larry Taylor walked into the hospital. He had told the family about the girl and wondered if he had made a mistake. Dr. Taylor knew the family would come for them. *Would they be safe?* He thought about it as he walked into his office and noticed a package on his desk. He had called the security office and asked for the footage of the north parking lot. He pushed the tape into the VCR and hit play. He fast-forwarded the video until he saw the old Dodge truck. He hit pause. He wrote down the number of the plates and called his friend at the DMV. Thirty minutes later, he parked his BMW across the road from Sandy's house. He watched as the twins brought boxes out of the house and loaded them on the back of the truck. He realized their intent. Sandy was going to take her twins and run.

He drove his car into the driveway and parked it behind the truck. As soon as the twins saw him, they ran inside the house. He got out of his car and stood beside it. One minute later, Sandy walked out of the house and sat down on the steps.

"Hello, Larry."

Larry walked over and sat beside her. "Where are you going?"

Sandy didn't answer his question. "How did you find me?"

"I work at the hospital. I watched the security tapes, made a phone call, and here I am." Larry stood up, reached down, and picked a rock up from the ground. He rolled it between his fingers. "Why, Sandy?" he asked. Sandy looked up at him.

"Why what?"

"Why was it so important to save that woman?"

"Even if it was just an accident, Carl shot her. We had to save her," Sandy said.

Larry sighed and looked at Sandy and started his rebuke. "Did you think about the camera? Didn't you know people would see the tapes? The kind of people who don't believe in the power of healing."

"Look, Larry. I know you don't understand this, but never in his life has Carl shown any type of emotion. He was so upset that he had shot the woman. I had to do something. And, no, at the time, I wasn't thinking about the consequences."

Larry threw the rock across the yard. "I called the family. They know you are here in Pine Level. Molly called me back. She and Ginger are on their way here. They want to help you," he said.

Sandy covered her face with her hands. "You know I don't trust them. It was Molly who tried to steal Carla from the hospital... It's why I ran," she said.

"Look at me, Sandy. There are tapes. People know. They saw the woman when they brought her into the hospital covered in her own blood. For God's sake, Sandy, the woman's lung was torn in half. She should have been dead before she reached the hospital. I was there when she died. I was dumbfounded when I was told she was alive, and even more so when they said she wasn't even shot. I couldn't figure it out until I saw the tapes. There's one tape that shows Carla going in and coming out of the woman's room. There is another tape showing the twins coming out of the hospital and getting into your truck. It shows you driving away. Now, I could have said, 'Hey! I know these people! They are my family. I have known about their power of healing all my life! But, no, sir, I didn't know they could raise the dead. Do you know what would have happened to me if I had said that? I would have been put in a straight jacket and hauled off to the nearest mental hospital," Larry said.

Sandy stood up. Tears ran down her face. "What do you want me to do?" she asked. "You and the twins stay here for now. I'll go back to the hospital and see if I can make this go away." He stood up and walked towards his car.

"Larry."

"Yes," he said without turning around.

"It's good to see you."

***

Paul left Sarah with his mother and father. He went back to the cabin, fixed the broken window, picked up the glass, and mopped up the blood. He tried to wrap his mind around the day's events but couldn't figure them out. Sarah had said she couldn't remember what had happened. He hoped that one day she would be able to tell him exactly what had unfolded that day. The sound of a car door closing caught his attention. Sarah and his mother walked into the cabin.

Anna stayed long enough to drink a cup of coffee. She wanted to stay longer, but Paul insisted she go home and check on his father. He walked her to her car. Anna opened the car door, then she turned around. "I just don't understand what happened, Paul. I saw the blood. I saw the hole in her breast. Now she acts like we are making this up. She thinks it's all a big joke."

Paul reached out and hugged his mother. "I can't explain it, either. I'm sure you saw what you said that you saw. I fixed the broken window and cleaned up the blood. We don't know how nor why any of this happened. You go on home, and as soon as I'm able to figure this out, I will call you."

Noon the next day, Paul walked out of the cabin and found Sarah sitting on their porch swing. He sat down beside her, reached over, and placed his hand on her leg. All of a sudden, Sarah jumped up. "Now I remember," she said. Then, she ran down the steps and across the yard.

"Where are you going?" Paul yelled.

"I know where they are!" Sarah yelled back as she ran around the lake.

Paul watched as Sarah disappeared into the woods. He ran inside the cabin and snatched his truck keys from the peg beside their back door. There was a dirt road that ran parallel with the property. If Sarah kept going, she would have to cross this road when she came out of the woods.

As soon as Paul turned down the dirt road, he remembered the old house. It had been empty for years. How could he have not known that someone had moved into it? He parked his truck on the road in front of the old house. Sarah stood beside an old Dodge truck, talking to a woman. A young boy and girl stood on the porch. After a few minutes, Sarah turned and walked back toward the road. Paul reached across the seat and opened the truck door. Sarah climbed in and closed the door. Paul turned the truck around, then drove back toward the highway. "What did she say?" he asked.

"She said it wouldn't work," Sarah said.

"What exactly is 'it'?" Paul asked.

"That little girl is 'it,' Paul. She has something neither you nor I nor anyone else around here can explain. It is true, Paul. I was dead, and that little girl somehow brought me back to life. And if she could do it for me, she can do it for others. Can't you see? No one has to die."

"Stop it, Sarah!" Paul yelled. "Think about what you're saying. People have to die. It's what keeps our world in balance," he said.

"If you are right, then tell me, Paul, why does this little girl have her gift?" Sarah asked.

"I don't know the answer to your question, but think about it, Sarah- If this little girl has what you call a 'gift', then don't you think others out there might have it, too? And don't you think they would know when and when not to use their gift?" Paul said.

Sarah thought about what Paul said. In her mind, she knew he was right, and Sandy was right. If this got out, then people would want to take her little girl away from her. And, yes, there had to be others like her.

"Are you coming inside?" Paul asked. It wasn't until then Sarah realized they were back at the cabin. "No, let's go for a walk," she said.

As they walked around the lake, she took Paul's hand in her own. Sarah told him everything. How she got out of bed, letting him sleep because she thought he would be hungover from the party. Taking a shower, then going into the kitchen to make coffee. She remembered looking out the window, seeing the deer and the boy holding the rifle, the window breaking, then the pain in her body. Sarah told Paul that she had called for him, and when he didn't answer, she grabbed what she thought were her car keys. She remembered going out into the rain, then realizing she had the keys to his truck. The last thing she remembered was seeing the twins running around the lake. Sarah stopped and turned, facing Paul. "This little girl is special. The boy shot me by accident. Now they may be in danger. Let's help them," she asked.

***

Molly pulled her car up next to the gas pumps in the small town of Coopers, Alabama. Ginger had been asleep in the back seat for the past three hundred miles. As soon as the car stopped, she opened her eyes. "Are we there yet?" she asked.

Molly looked back and smiled. "No, not yet, but we are close. We need gas, and I want to call Larry." She reached inside her purse and took out her wallet. She handed Ginger two twenties. "Here, take these, pay for the gas and grab us something to snack on," she said.

Ginger walked inside the store. Molly placed the pump nozzle inside the gas tank, then dialed Larry's number. After three rings, a woman's voice came on the line. "Dr. Taylor's office," she said.

"Let me speak to Larry," Molly said. The line went dead for a few seconds.

"Hey, Molly. Where are you?" he asked.

"How did you know it was me?"

"No one else would have called me Larry."

"We are in a small town called Coopers," Molly said.

"Good. You are about six miles from where we will meet. I want you to keep going south. You will see Highway 143. Turn left, and a half-mile down, you will come to a confederate cemetery. I'll be there in an hour."

"See you then," Molly said.

Ginger got back into the car. "What did Larry say?" she asked.

"Said he would meet us down the road. "What'd ya get us to eat? Molly asked.

"Cheese crackers and bologna."

"Sounds good to me," Molly said.

Larry pulled his BMW through the gates of the old cemetery. Molly looked at her watch. "Right on time," she said.

Before saying a word, Larry hugged both girls. "How are y'all doing?" he asked.

"We're okay. It's good to see you, Larry. Have you talked to Sandy?" Molly asked.

Before Larry could answer her question, the old Dodge truck pulled up beside them. Sandy and the twins got out. Carla walked over and took Ginger's hand in her own. "Let's go for a walk," Ginger said.

Once they were out of earshot so the others couldn't hear her, Carla let go of Ginger's hand. "You're like me, ain't you?" she asked.

Ginger knelt on one knee. "How did you know?" Ginger asked instead of answering Carla's question.

Carla paused, tilting her head to the side, then asked another question. "You and I have to go somewhere and hide, don't we?"

"Now, why would you ask such a question?" Ginger asked.

"I heard Mother and the woman talking. They said people would not understand our gift. They said people would take us away and lock us up," Carla said.

"They told you I would also be locked up?" Ginger asked.

"Not you. Me. But I thought since you and I are alike, they would lock you up, too," Carla said.

"You still haven't answered my question. How is it you know I also have the gift?" Ginger asked.

"You told me the day I was born. You were the first to hold me. You said one day you and I would be able to help a lot of people," Carla said.

At that moment, Ginger remembered picking Carla up and saying those exact words, but there should be no way for a newborn to remember. It was evident that this twelve-year-old girl's powers went far beyond what the family would understand. It had taken Ginger twenty-eight years to realize her potential. It was then that she remembered Carla's question.

"No, sweetheart. We are not going to hide from anyone. We have a home in Kentucky. There, we will be safe," Ginger said.

***

Two weeks later, Sarah came out of the woods in front of the old house. There were no curtains on the windows. It looked as if no one had lived there in years, but she knew better. A couple of weeks ago, she had stood in the yard talking to Sandy. A BMW was parked in the drive. A man she recognized sat on the porch.

"What are you doing here?" she asked.

"I bought the place, and you?" Larry asked. It was then that Sarah realized Dr. Larry Taylor knew something about the little girl.

"I believe she could-" Larry held up his hand, stopping Sarah in mid-sentence.

"Don't you think what you have in mind has already been tried?" he asked.

"Yes, but…" Once again, Larry held up his hand.

"There are no 'buts,' Sarah. Think about the girl. You have to let this go," he said.

"What about all of the people who know?" Sarah asked.

"I have destroyed the tapes and told the newspaper people that it was a practical joke you and I played on your husband. I was on my way to your house to let you know, but I stopped here, first," Larry said.

"How did you know them?" she asked.

"They are my family," Larry said.

Sarah went home and called Anna and Earl, inviting them to dinner. While they ate, she explained to them the best she could how and why they would never be able to tell anyone of their ordeal. They all agreed never to speak of the incident again; but, as time went on, they realized this would be impossible.

***

One hundred and twenty-five years later, Sarah sat on the old cabin's front porch looking down at the lake. She looked the same as she did the day Carla raised her from the dead. Over the years, she had located Sandy and met her whole family. Sandy, Molly, Larry, Ginger, and Carla had long passed on. Sarah raised her head as Carl walked toward the cabin holding a stringer of fish.

"What's on your mind, child?" Maw Maw Mindy asked. Sarah looked over at her and smiled.

"I was just wondering if you, Carl, and I are the only three people on this planet who will never die," she said.

CHOOSING DEATH

CHAPTER 3

*H*e sat on a limb in one of the many oak trees in her backyard. He could smell her blood. His senses were keen. He could pick out a single drop of blood, follow it throughout her body, and know the exact moment it re-entered her heart.

He is a young recruit, but so am I. It's amazing to me how much control he had over the thirst. It's been six months, and he is yet to kill a human. He lives off the blood animals. His lust for the young girl goes far beyond the thirst for her blood. It's her beauty that has him captivated. He has never in his life wanted anything, nor anyone, so badly. And yet, he doesn't understand why. At this moment, I am in his head. He doesn't know I am there. If he did, he would be angrier with me than he already is. I pray that one day he will understand why I had to turn him.

***

Three days after their grandmother's death, Britt D. sat across from his brother, Raymond.

"What did you say?" Britt asked

"I said it looks like the rain has stopped."

"No, before that," Britt stated.

"I said if our grandmother hadn't died, we wouldn't be in this mess.'"

"That's what I thought you said. Let me tell you something, buddy. It wasn't her fault, and I don't ever want to hear you say anything like that again! Do you hear me? I'm going to ask you one more time - do you hear me, Raymond?" Britt yelled at his brother.

"Yeah, yeah. I hear you," Raymond said.

Britt and Raymond Darbouze lived on the outskirts of Cordova, a small town in middle Alabama. Their parents, both mother, and father, had died while the boys were very young. Their grandmother from their mother's side of the family raised them. Maddy Ann Price had been well known and well respected in her community... until the ordeal began.

"She couldn't take it. Her heart gave out," Britt said.

"I know, I was there, and it was me who told-" Britt interrupted Raymond before he could finish his statement.

Holding his hand up and shaking his head, he looked at Raymond disbelievingly, "Let's not go there. You know I don't believe you," Britt said.

"Yeah, it's sad you don't, but the worst part of this ordeal is that no one else believes me, either," Raymond mentioned and went silently inward with his thoughts.

Standing to his feet, after some time had passed, Raymond walked over to the window. The clouds were fading away. The sun had gone down behind the trees.

"It's going to happen again, and when it does, they will come looking for me," he said.

Raymond had been standing by the window no more than a few minutes. A man in a long gray coat walked by for the second time. Both times, the man had stopped and looked up at him. He ran to the front door and out into the street. The man was nowhere in sight.

Raymond's thoughts went back to his grandmother. On the night of her death, Raymond found her at the top of the stairs. He wrapped his arms around her. Before she died, she told him about the man in the gray coat and what he had done to the Peterson family. Raymond walked down the stairs with caution. There were no bodies. Finding a single red dot on one of the chairs, he touched it with the tip of his finger. Realizing it was blood, Raymond wiped it on the sleeve of his jacket. One of the policemen noticed the stain, and now the whole town believed that he and his poor dead grandmother were responsible for the death of the entire Peterson family.

***

She must have felt his presence, but when she turned around, she saw no one. He is good. Even better than me. It was the sound of his feet hitting the ground that caused me to look. I watched him run across the yard, climb the side of her house, and enter through her bedroom window. He stood behind her. I watched as he bent forward to smell her hair. She wore a see-through, silk gown. The curves of her body were breathtaking. The material clung to her small breasts as if she were naked. He reached out to touch her. She started to turn. He disappeared around the side of her house. He was going to feed.

***

Raymond stood by the door with his suitcase in hand. "Where are you going?" Britt asked.

"I don't know. Far away from here. You saw the mob outside our house last night. They think I am him." Raymond answered.

"Who is he?" Britt responded.

"You didn't believe me before... why should I trust you to believe me now?" Raymond said.

"Listen to me, Raymond. Put yourself in my shoes. None of this has made any sense to me from the start." Britt hesitated for a few moments. "Okay... hell, Raymond, it's not that I don't believe you. It's just that I don't want to believe any of this is possible - much less true," he said.

Raymond set his suitcase down on the floor, walked over, and stood by the fireplace. Even though the house was warm, he felt a chill throughout his body. He turned, facing his brother.

"Last night, when I came out of the club, I saw him. I'm talking about the man in the gray coat. I followed him for several blocks. Finally, he approached one of the women who stood peddling her wares. He led her into an alley. At first, I thought he was kissing her neck, but she fell to the ground when he stepped back. I don't know if he knew I was there or if he knew that I saw what he had done. I yelled, but by the time I reached the woman, he had gone. I knelt and lifted her head. Her eyes were wide open, and her skin was the color of snow. I realized she was dead and that he had drunk her blood."

Britt shook his head from side to side. "So, brother, how did the mob come about chasing you? And how did you manage to get away from them?" he asked.

Raymond walked back toward the door. "I knew you wouldn't believe me. I have told you the truth. If you don't believe this, then there is no way you are going to believe how I got away from the mob," he said.

Britt stepped in between his brother and the door. "Look, Raymond, you know I will do whatever I can to help you. Please sit and tell me what happened," he said.

Britt went into the kitchen. He came back, holding two glasses of wine. He handed one of them to Raymond. The two of them sat on the couch. Raymond took a sip of the wine before he spoke.

"A policeman walked by the alley. When I yelled for help, he blew his whistle. Several people came running toward me; one man yelled my name. He called me a murderer. Someone else yelled, 'get him,' and I ran. Even though I didn't come here, the mob did. They knew where I lived."

"Where did you go?" Britt asked.

"This is where I need you to keep an open mind. If this hadn't happened to me, I wouldn't believe it myself. I ran past our house, turned down the block, then circled back through the alley across the street. It was like I was flying. The next thing I knew, I sat on the rooftop of the house across the street. The man in the gray coat sat next to me and held onto my arm. His touch was as cold as ice. I can still feel the chills running through my body. He told me not to worry. He would not let anyone hurt me for something that he had done. Then, I felt his hand leave my arm. He disappeared... like -poof- he was gone. I waited until the mob left, then climbed down the gutter drain and came home. So now you understand. I have to leave this town, and it has to be today."

Britt didn't say another word. Raymond stood up, walked over, and picked up his suitcase. Without looking back, he walked out the door.

***

I didn't hear or see him when he came back. I was in deep thought. I just happened to look up, and he was there.

I knew he would return; it is the very reason I didn't leave. He had to satisfy his thirst. What animal? A sheep or maybe a small goat? I could smell the blood. I pray he doesn't go back inside her room. If he does, he will know I was there. Although I was tempted, I didn't touch her. I wanted to turn her. For him, not me. I knew if I turned her, I would push him further away from me. He doesn't understand - I love him. The light will come soon. He will go to our home. He will not wait for me. It will be like every morning. He will be asleep when I return.

***

As soon as Raymond walked into the train station, he realized his mistake. Two men walked toward him. First, there was pain, second light, and then darkness.

When he opened his eyes, he was alone with the pain radiating in his head. His arms and legs were tied to a chair. He could hear voices in another room.

"Are you sure it's him?" a man asked.

"Yes, I'm sure. His name is Raymond Darbouze. He lives on Ninth Street. The house belongs to the old woman who died in the Peterson house," a second man said.

The next voice he heard came from a woman. "Do you think he killed her, too?" she asked.

The first man answered her question. "He could have, but the doctor said she died of heart failure. I believe she saw what he did to those people and couldn't take it," he said.

Raymond lost track of who was talking. The pain in his head got worse.

"Did you see the bodies?" "All but one. There were four in the basement." "The oldest daughter is missing." "What is her name?" "Peggy, Lynn." "Yes, isn't she supposed to be in college somewhere up north?" "Yes, but I checked. They are on some kind of break. She came home last week."

"Hello, out there! Why are you doing this to me? I haven't done anything!" Raymond yelled.

The door in front of him opened. "I see you are awake," the woman said.

"I heard you talking. I didn't hurt anyone," Raymond said.

She walked over and stood in front of him. "My name is Amy Barker. These are my brothers, Billy and Donald." She reached out, picked up Raymond's chin, and put her face close to his. "We are from Jackson, Mississippi. We are looking for the one who killed our sister," she said.

Raymond jerked his head to one side, causing her to release his chin.

"Look, lady. I heard what you said in there. I didn't kill the Petersons, nor that woman in the alley, and I swear to you I have never been to Jackson, Mississippi, in my life," he said.

"You were seen at both crimes," Donald said.

"Yes, I went to the Petersons to pick up my grandmother. I found her at the top of the stairs," Raymond said.

"And she was already dead?" Donald asked.

"No, she told me about a man in a gray coat. A few days later, I saw him walking by our house, then again on Fifth Street, when I came out of the club. I followed him into the alley where he killed that woman." Raymond noticed the two men look at one another. "It's him you are looking for, isn't it? You already knew I didn't kill those people. Untie me from this chair right now!" Raymond yelled.

"Yes, you are right. It is him we are looking for," Amy said.

"Then, what do you want from me?" Raymond asked.

Billy walked over and stood in front of him.

"Look, boy. We know what this man is. We know he doesn't come out in the daylight hours, which means someone is helping him, and we believe that someone is you. So why don't you do yourself a favor and tell us where he is?"

Before Raymond could answer, Billy punched him in the face. Amy grabbed Billy, pulling him away, and she shouted, "Give the boy a chance to talk!"

***

I asked if he was going to see the girl. He turned his back to me. I told him he could turn her. He turned around and stated that he would kill me in my sleep if I went near the girl. I smiled and assured him that when the time came, it would be him who turned her. He walked out the door like a normal human. I followed at a distance. He stopped, checked on the girl, then went to a nearby farm. Once he had finished feeding, he returned to his perch in the tree. I darted in and out of his mind.

He never knew it was me who put the image in his head. The girl stood naked before a mirror, readying herself for sleep; he watched as she laid upon the bed. He saw himself above her. Her head tilted, calling him to surrender. His endurance broke, and lust took over as she presented the object of his greatest desire: her throbbing veins beneath the surface of her neck. He saw his own sharp teeth as they sank into her pink flesh. He felt the sensation and power as he drank her blood.

He flew out of the tree, across the yard, and down the street. Once again, I followed him. I saw the sturdy, built woman. I saw the bag of groceries as it fell to the sidewalk. "At last, a human," I thought to myself. In an instant, he was gone. I walked over, looking down at the woman, her eyes opened, and her mouth moved. He had left her alive. I killed her myself. If I had not, she would have turned.

***

"He doesn't know anything. If you don't stop, he will die," Donald said.

Amy touched Billy on his shoulder. "He is right. We are wasting our time. Cut him loose," she said.

"What are we going to do with him?" Donald asked.

Billy reached out and cut the ropes. Raymond fell to the floor.

"Leave him. If he dies, so be it. I still believe, somehow, this boy is connected to him," he said.

Raymond's left eye was swollen shut. Rolling onto his back and his head tilting to the side, blood poured from his nose and mouth. Forcing himself into a sitting position, someone helped him to his feet. From the touch of his hand, Raymond knew it was the man in the gray coat. He turned to face him.

"Why me?" he asked.

"I told you I wouldn't let them hurt you for my sake," the man said.

Raymond spat a glob of blood onto the floor. "You're a little late, don't you think? And you still haven't answered my question. Why me?" he asked again.

The man handed Raymond a small piece of paper with an address written on it. "Go here while you have the cover of night. You will be safe. Wait until I return, then I will answer your question," he said.

Raymond made his way out of the house and onto the street. The pain in his head was almost unbearable. The address the man had given him was several blocks away. By the time he reached the house, his eyes were swollen to where he could barely see. Raymond realized he stood in front of the town's largest house, standing four stories tall. Before he could knock, the door opened before him. Raymond stepped inside the house. A strange-looking man wearing a dark suit caught him before he hit the floor.

Raymond felt the covers atop him, opening his eyes. He lay in a four-poster bed. There was a plate of food and a glass of wine sitting on a small table beside him. He reached over the food, picked up the glass of wine, and drank it down in one swallow. When he slid out of bed, he stood naked on the cold, hard wooden floor. His clothes had been washed, folded, and placed in a neat pile on the foot of the bed. He quickly dressed, then exited the room. He found himself on the third floor of the big house. He walked down the stairs, then wandered around the first floor.

Raymond wandered into the kitchen and saw the man in the dark suit standing over a sink, washing a pot. He looked up as Raymond entered the room.

"Would you like some more wine?" he asked.

Without giving Raymond time to answer, he dried his hands on a dishtowel, walked over to a cabinet, took out a bottle of wine, poured a tall glass, and handed it to him.

"How do you know Sir Edgar?" the man asked.

"It's not him, I know. I know what he does, or should I say, what he did." Raymond pointed to his face. "It's because of him that this happened to me. He sent me here and asked me to wait until he returned. Do you know when this will be?" he asked.

"You say you know what he does, then you must know he is here now, yet he sleeps. He will awake soon. Until then, my name is Patrick, and I am at your service, Sir…. your name, Sir?" Raymond thought of a fake name but decided to tell the man the truth.

"My name is Raymond, Raymond Darbouze," he said.

"Would you care for something to eat, Sir Raymond?" Patrick asked.

"No, thank you. Right now, I am going to take a look around this big house," he said.

One hour later, Raymond stood on the fourth floor. "There must be at least sixty rooms in this house," he thought to himself.

"Seventy-three in all, counting the basement," came a voice from behind him. Raymond spun around. The man in the gray coat was standing behind him. Instead of a gray coat, he, too, now wore a dark suit. He stepped back, waved his arm in a downward motion, then bowed.

"Sir Edgar Renard at your service," he said.

***

When I entered our sleep chamber, he sat on his bed. I put the image of the sturdy woman in his head. He saw he had left her alive. He saw me as I knelt, clamping my hand over her mouth. He saw her hand come up, scratching at my face. He saw her head turn backward as I broke her neck. It was then I spoke. "Do you understand why I had to do this," I asked?

He didn't answer but just looked at me. I was still in his head, and he was confused, so I took him back to the beginning.

He saw himself holding the fat woman. He saw her fall to the ground. He saw her lying alone with her eyes opened. He saw a man, woman, and child walking down the street. I skipped over the formalities. He saw the man and woman lying on the ground. He saw the fat woman holding the child with its neck ripped out. I asked if he now understood. He nodded his head, then laid down to sleep. I watched him sleep. The night came fast.

This night, it was he who followed. Out of my own curiosity, I led him to the farm, then stood beside a small calf. He shook his head. I led him back into town. We stood in the shadows behind a club. A man and woman came out, and we watched as they kissed. The woman raised her dress as the man stepped behind her. I reached over and touched his arm. I took the man, and he took the woman. I watched as he finished feeding. He broke the woman's neck before dropping her to the ground. He looked at me. It was the first time I had seen him smile since I had turned him.

***

Raymond sat across the table from the man he now knew as Sir Edgar. For reasons unknown to himself, he felt excitement. He had read many books about people like Sir Edgar, but never in his wildest dreams had he believed they were real.

"You have a question?" Sir Edgar asked. Raymond picked up the glass of wine Patrick had set in front of him. He took several sips before he spoke.

"How old are you?" he asked.

"Ah… always the first question. I was born in Rome, Italy, a little over three thousand years ago. I lived as a mortal for sixty-five years before I was turned. I will remain this mortal age until I die," he said.

"I thought people like you were immortal, so what do you mean when you say 'until you die'?" Raymond asked.

"No one is immortal. Some just last longer than others. People like me will not suffer what you call 'a natural death', but we can be killed," Sir Edgar said.

"How many others like you are there?" Raymond asked.

"Many thousand," Sir Edgar said.

"How can you be killed?" Raymond asked. Sir Edgar looked over at Raymond and smiled.

"Do you have plans for my death?" he asked.

"No, no, no. I'm not interested in your death. On the contrary, it's your life that fascinates me. I want to be like you," Raymond said. Sir Edgar let out a long, loud laugh.

"You wish that I turn you?" he asked.

"Yes, but why do you think it's funny?" Raymond asked.

"How old are you?" Sir Edgar asked.

"I'm twenty-one in a month," Raymond said.

"And you wish to remain twenty-one?" Sir Edgar asked.

"My age doesn't matter. It's the future I'm interested in. I want to see what happens for the next thousand years," he said.

Sir Edgar stood to his feet. "I will tell you what your future will hold for the next thousand years. Even in this state of life, our true emotions stay intact. You will fall in love with women and men many, many times, only to watch them grow old and die. Some of them you will turn, only to watch them lose interest in you and partake in their own journey. Some, you will kill yourself. The Drags will kill some. Never again will you know what it's like to watch the sun come up in the morning, and every night the thirst will come. At first, one kill will satisfy you, but in time, one hundred will not." He bent over and placed both hands on the table, looking Raymond in his eyes. "Do you still wish to be turned?" he asked.

"Who are the Drags you spoke of?" Raymond asked.

"They are mere mortals who have been killing people like me since before I was turned. They are smart. We rarely know who they are. They are called the Drags because it's what they do. They have a special rope, and when they have it around our feet, they drag us into the fire," he said.

"So, you die by fire," Raymond said.

"Among other ways. I'm sure you have read in the fictional books people write about us; fire, the sunlight, a wooden stake through the heart, and beheading. All are true. In time, for some of us, death is good. Some will use sunlight. Some will let the Drags catch them, while some recruit other people to kill them. You have asked the question, 'why you'?"

Sir Edgar tilted his head to one side. Raymond stood up and stepped back from the table.

"Are you saying you wish for me to kill you?"

***

I awoke from my sleep. It was night. He had already left our chamber. I went into town and fed. He, too, had been there. I could smell him. Knowing where he would be, I went there myself. Once again, he was inside her room. She wasn't there. He laid on her bed. I wanted to go in and lay beside him. I was afraid he would get angry. Over the past few nights, I had made progress in earning his trust. I didn't want to push him away from me again. I wanted him to love me as he had once before. He was mortal then, yet so was I. Even after I was turned, he vowed to love me until he died. I wish now I had never turned him.

He is back on his perch. She has entered her room. He watched as she undressed. She turned to face the window. It was as if she looked into his eyes as she slid the silk gown over her head. I waited for him to leave before I went to her.

The morning came. We were inside our sleep chamber. He came to me. We made love for hours. I knew he thought of her, so I entered his head. I allowed him to see the two of us before we were turned. He didn't speak. He lay next to me until night. I was still in his head. He was going to turn her. I had to leave. I knew not what to expect from him, for I knew he would find her dead.

***

Sir Edgar sat back down in his chair. "Yes, I am asking you to kill me. The Drags who hurt you no longer live. I took care of them myself. You may also have this house. Patrick will take care of the paperwork. He, too, will stay as long as you wish. He is a good servant."

Raymond sat back down. Sir Edgar reached over and touched his hand. "I wish this to be done tonight," he said. Raymond looked Sir Edgar in his eyes.

"I will accept your offer and do as you bid, but you must also do as I ask. I wish to be turned," Raymond said. Sir Edgar stood and walked toward the door. Without turning around, he spoke. "As you wish."

***

I walked through the graveyard, thinking of him. I didn't know such a thing was possible, as a tear fell from my eye. Five graves were before me, mother, father, brother, sister, and even though they didn't find my body, a grave for me. I lay on top of it. Someone will find my ashes. I saw the sun as I looked up and read my headstone.

In Loving Memory
Peggy Lynn Peterson

LOST YEARS

CHAPTER 4

It all started on a Sunday. The temperature was in the triple digits for the fifth day in a row. I ended my morning fishing trip early because, by nine a.m., the fish were not hungry, or they had gone where the water might be a little cooler. I docked my ten-foot Jon boat alongside my pier instead of inside the boathouse for fear that the heat penetrating the tin roof might cause the gas tank to explode.

After venturing into the house, turning on the television only to find out the race in Richmond had been rained out, I decided to take a ride through the country. I packed a cooler with bottles of water, Dr. Pepper, and a six-pack of Miller beer. I hardly ever drank and drove, but thought 'what the heck.' I would be driving down a dirt road where hardly anyone ever went. I loaded the cooler in my new Ford F150 and set out on my journey. I took the new cell phone my granddaughter had given me for my fifty-eighth birthday out of my shirt pocket and lay it on the seat beside me. She taught me how to use the camera. I thought maybe I could snap some pictures of wild animals, like rabbits or deer and perhaps even a bobcat if I was lucky.

I guess I was about two hours into my journey. The air conditioner had cooled the temperature inside the truck to around sixty degrees. With the outside heat forgotten, I had taken several pictures. Two of a rabbit, one of a doe escorting her fawn across the dirt road, and the prize of them all was one of a red fox. I had drunk two of the beers and decided not to chance to drink another. Instead, I reached inside the cooler and wrapped my hand around my drink of choice. It was then that I saw her. She looked to be in her mid-fifties, with long salt and pepper hair. She wore a long-sleeved dress, which almost dragged the ground when she walked. She was pushing a bicycle with big, knobby tires and a wire basket attached to the handlebars. At that very moment, I realized three things. First, and most importantly, pain, letting me know that I still had my hand wrapped around the soda and had yet to pull it out of the ice. So, I let go of the can and snatched my hand out of the cooler. Second, I realized the back tire on the woman's bike was flat. And third, the poor woman was soaked in her own sweat from the outside heat.

I pulled the truck a little ways past her before I stopped. I took a bottle of water from the cooler then stepped out of the truck. The woman had stopped. She had this strange look on her face. I couldn't tell if it came from fear or frustration.

"I'm not going to hurt you. I just want to help," I said. I twisted the cap off the bottle of water and held it out in front of me. "You look like you could use this," I said. The woman said one word.

"Yes." Using her foot, she pushed down on the bike kickstand, leaving it where it stood. She walked over, reached out, and took the water from my hand.

She drank almost half, then poured some in her hands and splashed it on her face. She said another word. "Hot."

"Yes, it is," I agreed with her. I opened the truck door.

"Why don't you sit in here and cool off," I said.

She tilted her head to one side. I couldn't tell if she was debating killing me or getting into the truck. I was relieved when she slid onto the seat. I closed the door, walked over, picked up her bike, and lay it in the back of my truck.

Once I was back inside the truck, I reached over and opened the cooler.

"I have water, Dr. Pepper, and beer," I said.

"Beer," the woman said. I took out a bottle of Miller, opened it, then handed it to the woman. She took a big swallow, and for the first time, I saw her smile.

"Good, uh?" I said.

"Yes, thank you," she said.

We rode in silence for a couple of miles. I watched her out of the corner of my eye. She had finished drinking the beer but held onto the bottle.

"Would you care for another?" I asked.

"No, thank you. I'm good. But you need to turn around," she said.

I looked over at her. It was then I realized that even at her age, she was naturally pretty. Her face was dark from too much sun, and her eyes were a light shade of green. I was guessing underneath her modest dress that she had an hourglass figure and weighed no more than one hundred and ten pounds. I realized she had said something. I also realized I had stopped the truck.

"I'm sorry, what did you say?" I asked.

"My house. It's in the opposite direction."

A little embarrassed and trying to play off my stupidity, I thought of her bike. "I know a place not far from here where we can get the tire fixed on your bike."

"I don't have any money with me."

"It's okay. I'll pay for it."

She sighed and looked at me and sternly stated, "Look, mister, I'm going to let you pay to have my bike fixed because it's the only transportation I have. But don't you be expecting any favors from me."

At first, I didn't understand what she meant by her statement, and once again, I felt stupid.

"Oh, no, you have it all wrong. I just want to help you... I don't want to have sex with you."

"What's the matter? You don't think I'm good enough for you?"

"No, it's not that. It's just that...." The woman started laughing.

"It's okay. I was just busting your chops. I do appreciate your help."

Another mile down the road, I realized one more thing. Neither she nor I had bothered to introduce ourselves. "My name is Robert Odell, but everyone calls me Robby."

Her smile reached her eyes as she acknowledged my name and introduced herself. "It's a pleasure to meet you, Robby. My name is…. Well, you can call me Jami," she said as her thoughts reflected upon the course of events that led to her sitting in the truck enjoying the cool of the air conditioner.

***

I met him on a Sunday, late morning just before midday. The weather was a lot hotter than where I'm from. The house I had rented did have an air conditioner in my small bedroom, so that's where I lived most of the time. But on this day, I decided to get out of the house. There was a store three miles away if I turned left when I exited my driveway and another eight miles if I turned right. Usually, ten times out of ten, I would have turned left on a day like today, but for some reason that I still haven't figured out, I turned right.

I had already traveled four of the eight miles when I knew I had made a mistake. The back tire on my bicycle went flat. I was already soaking wet with sweat. I had worn a long-sleeved, full-length dress to keep me from getting sunburned, and now, pushing my bike instead of riding it, my dress didn't help matters. But the walk did give me time to think back on all the events that started this whole ordeal.

I'm jumping way ahead; let me speak honestly. My real name is Sandra Leann Champion, but I had rented the house under the name Jami Edwards. I was born and raised in New York but went to college down here in the south at Auburn University in Lee County, Alabama. It all happened after I had graduated and moved back to New York.

I was walking on the sidewalk heading to apply for a job working as a child psychologist for the state of New York. I noticed several people pressing their faces against the window outside the studio of a famous news broadcast that was being aired live. Wondering what was going on, I, too, walked over and pressed my face against the glass. I didn't recognize anyone special, except for the same two women and a man I had watched several mornings on my television. I looked up into the camera, which seemed to be pointed directly at my face, and I remember that sent chills down my spine. Trying to shake the strange feeling from my mind, I turned and walked away as fast as I could. At that time, it wasn't very fast because it seemed like everyone and their brothers were on their way to work, and all were traveling down the exact same sidewalk.

I had made it a little over two blocks when a man handed me an envelope. I remember the man's exact words.

"Excuse me, miss. I've been trying to catch up to you. I saw you drop this on the last block." Before I could protest and tell the man he'd made a mistake, he disappeared into the crowd.

When I looked, I was shocked to see my name typed in caps on both sides of the envelope. Thinking someone must be playing some kind of joke, I almost, well I did, drop it inside a trash bin. But, before walking away, my curiosity got the best of me. I reached down and retrieved the envelope and read the letter inside.

I saw you look into my eyes. I have chosen you. It could be for the better or the worst, and your participation will be your choice. Check your phone. Call the last number on the list at precisely six p.m. tomorrow. Don't be early nor late. A lifetime experience depends on your punctuality.

I wove my way through the crowd and hailed a cab. Instead of my job interview, I went straight home. Once inside my apartment, I reread the letter ten times. I checked my phone and wrote the number down at the bottom of the message in case my phone just happened to go on the blitz at or before six p.m. tomorrow.

My mind was thinking more than one hundred thoughts a second. I couldn't imagine who had sent this letter, nor why it was sent to me. I knew I needed to do something to calm my mind, so I took the next step in mind control, only this step gave power to another source. I walked into my kitchen, took down a bottle of Jim Beam, and screwed the cap off. Not bothering to get a glass, I drank from the bottle.

I don't remember much more of that day. I awoke the next day around noon. I took a shower before going into the kitchen for coffee.

The empty Jim Beam bottle sat on the floor beside the table. Just looking at the bottle made my head hurt, so I picked it up and threw it in the trash. I forced myself to eat an egg sandwich and drink three strong cups of coffee. My mind started on another rampage. I looked at the clock on my stove. It was one-thirty p.m., four and a half hours to kill before I could make the call. A half-hour later, I found myself sitting on a bench in Central Park watching the pigeons fight over bread crumbs a little girl was throwing on the ground.

My thoughts went back to 'why' and 'who,' but no reason or person came to mind. The next time I looked at my watch, it read five fifty-five p.m. I picked up my phone as I took a deep breath to calm my heightened sense of nervousness. Scrolling down my saved contacts, I found and stared at the number as I patiently waited the last five minutes before hitting the call button. A man answered with "Hello?" on the second ring. "Tell me your name," he said.

"You already know my name. It was written on the envelope," I said.

"If you refuse to answer my questions, I will move on, and you will never know if you made the right choice," he said.

"My name is Sandra Leann Champion."

"And your age?"

"Twenty-eight next week," I said.

"At what age would you like to retire?"

"I haven't really thought about retirement. Hell, I don't even have a job, but I guess around twenty-five years from now would make me fifty-three," I said.

"This is a question you must think about before you give me your answer. Remember, your choice could be for the better, or it could be for the worse. The question is, would you like to live the next twenty-five years of your life, remembering everything you see or hear? Go home to your apartment. Your second letter sits beside your door. If you choose not to participate., you will never hear from me again."

Before I was able to ask him anything else, he disconnected the call. Instead of hailing a cab, I ran the twenty-nine blocks back to my apartment. I found a small box with an envelope taped to the top.

I don't know why, but I looked around to be sure there was no one around before picking up the box. I unlocked the door, went inside, sat the box on my coffee table, and then sat down on the couch. I was so nervous my hands were shaking. I managed to get the letter out of the envelope without tearing it.

> *"If you would like to live the next twenty-five years of your life in one night, follow these instructions: Get dressed for bed. Inside the box, you will find a small bottle that contains a powerful potion. Drink all of it before laying down to sleep. If, on this day, your clock goes past midnight, the potion will no longer work. Read the sentence that I underlined to make sure you understand its meaning."*

My mind went back and forth. I read the entire letter ten times. I didn't catch the meaning of the underlined sentence until I awoke the next day. It was fifteen minutes until midnight when I drank the potion. It was like any other dream, except I could remember every detail of what seemed like a normal life. I had worked for the state of New York for twenty of the twenty-five years. I never married but had several boyfriends. I remember the sex being good with some and not so good with others. I went to baseball games by myself—an everyday life for a strong-minded, independent woman.

The sound of the approaching truck brought my mind back to reality. I pushed my bike as far to the side of the road as I could without stepping into a ditch. The truck moved past me at a slow pace. The man inside looked as if he couldn't make up his mind if he wanted to stop or keep going. Although I was a little leery, I was hoping he would stop. I knew my hopes had been accepted by the universe when I saw the brake lights on the truck. I wanted to smile but held a stern look on my face. He got out of his vehicle, held up his hand, and said he wasn't going to hurt me. He never noticed my hand inside my purse wrapped around the handle of a twenty-five-stocked barrel pistol.

He held out a bottle of water. I drank some, then splashed some on my face. Once inside the truck, he offered three choices of something else to drink—water, Dr. Pepper, or beer. I chose beer. I didn't speak for a while. I knew I would have to tell him he needed to turn around because my house was in the opposite direction from which we were traveling, but I wanted to enjoy as much of the cold air as possible. When I finally did tell him, he informed me we were going someplace where my flat tire could be fixed. Although I had my own money, I told him I didn't. When he said he would pay for the repairs himself, I let him know he shouldn't expect any favors from me. When he assured me he didn't expect any, I decided to mess with his head, but he figured it out when I laughed.

He told me his name was Robert, but I could call him Robby. I didn't ask his age; I figured around sixty. He had a bald head but sported a goatee. He wore nice clothes, and the truck was new, so I figured he could afford the few dollars it would take to get the bike repaired. I lied when I told him my name was Jami and knew he could never guess I was only twenty-nine years old.

***

Robby stopped his truck in front of the only service station in the small town of Clanton, Alabama. "You can wait inside the truck where it's cool," he said.

Sandra nodded her head and watched the man. At the time, she didn't know he would do a lot more to help her as he unloaded the bike and pushed it into the service station. Once again, Sandra thought of her situation. She had found the third letter on her nightstand the morning she awoke in a body twenty-five years older than it should be. It was her first clue in finding the man who had done this cruel thing to her.

She kept her eyes on Robby as he talked to a tall, slim man wearing grease-covered overalls. Three statements entered her mind—the underlined sentence in the second letter.

"If you would like to LIVE the next twenty-five years of your life in one night."

The second statement was the clue she had found taped to the outside of the door of her apartment five minutes after she had called the number and left an angry message. "An Eagle and Tiger are one. You have already been there, but it was for fun. You must live there a year if you want to return to a life which should have been when you were already young."

It had taken less than a minute to figure out the clue. The Eagle and Tiger were mascots at Auburn University, where she had gone to college. The old house in which she lived is where she and some of her friends would party. Today made one year, so somewhere, somehow, she would receive another clue. The third statement came from Robby. "I'm not going to hurt you. I only want to help." She sure hoped he meant it. Robby told the man at the service station to do whatever it took to fix the bike, and he would return in about an hour to pick it up. He saw the woman he knew as Jami watching his every step as he approached the truck. Not knowing what he had gotten himself into, he opened the door and slid into the seat.

"The mechanic said it would be ready in an hour. I know a place not far from here where we can get something to eat. How does that sound?"

"Yes, I could use a sandwich about now."

As Robby pulled the truck out onto the highway, a car with New York plates pulled into the service station. Sandra didn't say anything, for she already knew what to expect.

"What do you do?" Sandra asked.

"Me, well, I'm twice retired. I live on a lake. I fish, swim, and watch TV. That's about it," Robby said.

"Where did you retire from?"

Robby realized the quiet time was over. Now this woman wanted to talk, and she wanted to talk about him, which he had no desire to do but knew he shouldn't be rude to someone he just met.

"Army National Guard and the state, and I was a high school science teacher."

Intrigued by his work choices, Sandra continued.

"So, are you one of those science teachers that believe in the Big Bang Theory?"

"Are you asking if I believe in evolution?" Robby asked.

"No, not necessarily evolution. Do you believe things are always as they seem, or do you believe in supernatural events?"

Curiously looking at her, "Do you mean ghosts and such?"

Sandra smiled, "No, not ghosts."

She knew it was a risk to speak her real thoughts. Would he be capable of accepting all that she had to say? He noticed her hesitation as she smiled and then continued with a statement that made him think.

"What if I told you I went to sleep one night, and when I woke up the next day, my body had aged twenty-five years. Would you think it possible?" Sandra asked.

Robby thought a few minutes before answering her question. "I believe this is a question that if I say yes, you would think I'm nuts, and if I say no, you would think that I believe you are nuts. So, what I would like to do here is plead the fifth," he said.

Quickly changing the subject, Sandra asked, "Where are we going to eat?"

"There is a barbeque place right up the road from here called Ted's. They have delicious sandwiches," Robby said.

They were almost finished eating when the man from the service station walked into the restaurant. He walked straight to their table and handed Sandra an envelope. As she was putting it inside her purse, Robby saw the name Sandra Leann Champion written on the envelope.

"A man from New York said he was sorry he missed seeing you in person, but he had to get back to New York. When he left that letter, he paid for having your bike fixed." He looked over at Robby. "I put it in the back of your truck."

The man started to walk away, then turned back, facing Sandra. "Oh yeah, I almost forgot. He said to tell you this one won't be as easy as the last," he said.

Robby watched him exit the restaurant.

Glancing at Sandra, "Do you know who he is talking about?"

Sandra shook her head. "I don't know him personally, but I know what he wanted. Do you know anyone who works for the police who might run a license number and not ask too many questions?" she asked.

"Yes, as a matter of fact, I do, but first things first… who is Sandra Leann Champion?" Robby asked.

Sandra stood up abruptly. "Let's get out of here, and I'll tell you everything."

They rode in silence. Sandra contemplated and organized her thoughts. It wasn't until they were back on the dirt road where they had met before she began to speak.

"My real name is Sandra Leann Champion. I was born and raised in New York. Remember the question I asked about going to bed young and waking up old? Well, it happened to me."

She went on to speak before Robby could answer her question. He drove at a slow pace, listening to every word, the first letter, the phone call, the second letter, and how the letter inside her purse contained the second clue.

Robby pulled the truck into the driveway of a small house when Sandra pointed toward it. He put the gear lever into park but left the engine running so the cool air would continue to blow from the vents. Looking at Sandra, Robby opened his mouth but couldn't find any words. So, he turned his head, staring out the windshield of his truck. Without looking at her, he began to talk.

"Okay, let's say I have an open mind, which I try to have in every situation, but I am now fifty-eight years old, and this is the most unlikely thing I have ever heard of. You say the envelope in your purse is the second clue, and the man sent word by the guy who fixed the flat tire on your bike that this clue wouldn't be as easy as the first. So, why do you seem so calm, and why haven't you looked at the second clue?" he asked.

Sandra shook her head. "I'm not as calm as it appears. Right now, I feel like screaming. I was waiting for you to drop me off before I read it."

Roddy's inner thoughts ran rapid. However, his subconscious mind, or maybe it was his attraction to the woman that took over. It made a decision as he heard himself say,

"Let's read it together."

Sandra reached inside her purse, brought out an envelope, and handed it to Robby. He unfolded the letter and read it aloud. She opened the door and stepped out of the truck.

"Wait, you asked if I had a friend who worked for the police department," Robby said.

"Yes, when we were leaving the service station, I believe I saw him." She reached inside her purse and took out a pen and small notepad. From memory, she wrote down the number of the New York license plate. She tore out the piece of paper and handed it to Robby. "Find out who owns this car."

Without saying another word, she closed the door, pulled her bike from the back, and pushed it toward the house. He waited until she was inside the house before backing out of the driveway.

***

Robby didn't believe in coincidence. He had gone along with Jami's, or Sandra's, or whatever her name might be, a story about the last twenty-five years of her life. After traveling a couple of miles down the dirt road, his cell phone rang. He stopped the truck and picked up his phone. The caller ID said Jack Carter, his friend from the police department. "What's up, buddy?" Jack asked.

"Nothing much." But what he really wanted to say was, "*Hey man, I've met this woman who claims to have lost twenty-five years of her life. I'm torn between believing that she is crazy or that she and some other people are trying to play a mean mind game with me.*"

"The wife and I are having a backyard cookout this Saturday. BYOB. You coming?" Jack asked. "As of now, I don't have plans, but things could change. I was on my way home and was going to call you when I got there. I need a favor," Robby said.

'Okay, bud, lay it on me."

"If I give you the number of a New York plate, can you find out who owns the car?" Robby asked. "Sure thing. As a matter of fact, I had to come in today, and I'm at my desk right now. Give me the number."

Robby read the number from the piece of paper that Sandra had given him.

"Hold on a minute," Jack said. It was less than a minute when Jack came back on the line. "The car belongs to the NBS news station in New York City," he said.

"NBS news?" Robby repeated.

"Yes, it doesn't say who drives the car. According to my information, the station owns fifty-one cars of different makes and models. The one you are looking for is a 2011 Mercedes. Hey, pal, what's this all about?" Jack asked.

"I really don't know yet. So far, no one has broken any laws. As soon as I find out, I'll call you back. As of now, I plan to be there Saturday," Robby said before disconnecting the call. He found a place where he could turn the truck around and drove back to Sandra's house.

When he pulled into her driveway, he saw her standing on the front porch. He watched as she walked out and got into the truck.

"We need to go. I figured out the first part of the clue," Sandra said.

"Don' you want to know why I came back?" Robby asked.

"Yes, but you can tell me on the way. We need to get to Auburn University before five-thirty," Sandra said. Robby looked at his watch.

"We still have two hours. It's not too far from here. We have plenty of time, so tell me about the first part of the clue," Robby said.

"You, first. Why did you come back?" Sandra asked.

"The car you saw, was it a 2011 Mercedes?".

"I'm not sure, I was focused on memorizing the plate number, but it could have been," Sandra said.

"The car belongs to the NBS news station in New York City. They own a lot of cars, so unless you're going back to New York, there's no way to find out who drives it," Robby said.

"I had a feeling it had something to do with them."

"Who is 'them'?" Robby asked.

Sandra told him about looking into the broadcasting station window. Then two blocks away, she had received the first letter. "I believe looking into that window was when it all started. I had a strange feeling when the camera was pointed directly in my direction."

"So, how does this and Auburn University tie together?" Robby asked.

"I can't answer that, and from what you just told me, I may be chasing a rabbit trail. The first part of the clue…

'Two hours, three days, listened but never talked'.

During my last year at Auburn, I needed one credit hour to obtain my master's degree in psychology. I took a course in science engineering, which at first consisted of machines that could do humans' work. Today, the same course would be called robotics. The class was two hours, three days a month, taught by Professor David Hallmart. He did all the talking. If we had questions, we had to either write them on paper or send him an email. Near the end of the course, he changed his entire curriculum from machines to chemicals. He believed he had found a formula for a fountain of youth. I still have some of his notes on my laptop," Sandra said.

"What makes you think Dr. Hallmart would target you?" Robby asked.

"During the course, I sent him an email telling him I didn't believe he was right. He gave me a C, barely allowing me to pass. I sent him another email calling him a crazy jerk," Sandra said.

"Call him," Robby said.

"What? Why?" Sandra asked.

"If you believe he is the first part of the clue, then he could also be the second *'I was here, but now gone.'*

"Use my phone and call the university," Robby said.

He listened to a one-sided call as Sandra called 411 asking for the number to Auburn University, then another when she was connected to the college.

"I would like to speak to Dr. David Hallmart. Oh, I see. Do you have a number where he might be reached? I see. Well, thank you for your time."

Sandra lay the phone down on the seat between them.

"He moved to New York eight months ago. The University more or less fired him for using his students for 'some kind of experiment'," she said.

Robby drove back to the small town of Clanton. He pulled up in front of a mini-mart store and went inside. When he got back into the truck, he reached inside a bag, brought out a tallboy can of Miller beer, and handed it to Sandra. She popped the tab and took a long swallow.

"Thanks, that's good," she said.

"We are going to New York," Robby said.

"Don't you have a life of your own?" Sandra asked.

"Yes, I do, and right now, at this point in time, I'm making you and this strange ordeal a part of it," he said.

"So, you believe me?" Sandra asked.

Robby pulled the truck back out onto the highway. "Let's just say I do believe something. I don't know if it's by accident, fate, or just plain chance you and I met today. I've always been ambitious, so I see this as a new adventure. So, now I'm asking you, do you want to go to New York or not?"

Sandra shook her head. "I can't ask you to go. All I know, at this point, is Dr. Hallmart is somewhere in New York. I have less than one thousand dollars to my name, which might last a week in New York if I eat light," she said.

Robby laughed, then reached over and touched her arm. "No one is going to eat light. I have lots of money with nothing to spend it on. This should solve one of your problems, so you can concentrate on where you believe we should start looking," he said.

"Okay, let's say I accept your help and your money: how are we going to 'solve the problem' of how to get ourselves to New York?" Sandra asked.

Again, Robby laughed. "We are sitting in it," he said.

"You are going to drive this truck to New York?"

"We go back to your house. You pack what you need. We go to my house. I pack a bag, we get some sleep, then leave before the sun comes up. Taking turns, we drive straight through, putting us in New York sometime day after tomorrow," he said.

This time it was Sandra who laughed. "New York, here we come," she said.

***

The drive had taken them twenty-two hours. Sandra pulled the truck into a parking deck in Queens. Robby woke up and looked around.

"Where are we?" he asked.

"Queens. We can leave your truck here. This place has security, so it'll be safe. From now on, we will use public transportation. It's a lot easier than trying to find parking spaces for the truck. I've already called and booked us a room at the Juliette Hotel near the NBS news station. It's a cheap place, only $450 a night," she said.

"Whatever you think we should do. I see you, and I have been thinking along the same lines. The letter came from a man driving a car which belongs to the news station, so we should start by finding who drives the Mercedes," Robby said.

"I'm one step ahead of you... and sorry about your truck." Before Robby could respond, Sandra got out of the truck, walked to the back, and delivered a backward mule kick to the fender leaving a softball-sized dent. Robby jumped out of the truck, looked at the dent, then leaned his head to one side.

"You called the police, told them you were hit by the Mercedes, gave them the plate number."

"And they are going to call me back and tell me who was driving the car," Sandra said, finishing his statement. Robby reached down and touched the dent. "Smart," he said.

Although there were empty seats, Robby stood holding on to one of the balance straps hanging from the roof. "First time on a subway?" Sandra asked.

He looked down where she sat and smiled. "How far?" he asked.

"We get off at the next stop."

Fifteen minutes later, Robby followed Sandra out onto the platform.

"Where to, now?" he asked. Before she had time to answer, his phone rang. He looked at the caller ID and handed the phone to Sandra.

"It's the police." Once again, he found himself listening to a one-sided conversation. "Hello? Yes, this is Sandra Champion. Yes, I called."

Robby watched as she fumbled through her purse and brought out her pen and notepad. Looking over her shoulder, he saw that she had already written down a name and was in the process of writing down an address.

"Thank you," she said before disconnecting the call. She looked into Robby's eyes and smiled. "Got him," she said. "Dr. Hallmart?" Robby asked.

"No, the man who drives the Mercedes. The police called NBS and got his name and address. And get this, I know him, or I knew him. He was in my class, and that's not all - he was Dr. Hallmart's student aide," she said.

"Okay, what now?" Robby asked.

"Right now, we go up top, hail a cab, and go to the hotel," Sandra said.

A half-hour later, Robby followed Sandra into the hotel suite. He looked around. The suite was larger than most houses back in Alabama. There was a large living room, a full kitchen, two bedrooms, and a bathroom bigger than his boathouse that held his pontoon and bass boat. Sandra looked at him.

"You can put those suitcases down, now," she said with a laugh.

"What do we do now?" he asked.

"You go ahead and shower, then I will. While your showering, I'm going to order some food and wine. After I eat, I'm going to get drunk, then get some sleep - in that order. There's no need to be in any big hurry. We know where he lives. We will go see him tomorrow," she said.

The next morning, Sandra ordered breakfast that was delivered to their suite. She laid out their plan.

"The man we are going to see, his name is Mark Ingram. Judging from the clue, I think we will find Dr. Hallmart next door, or he may even be in the same house when we get there. I've already called a cab. It will be downstairs in a half-hour. We will backtrack to your truck, then drive over to the ferry. The house we are looking for is on Long Island."

***

Robby stood at the rail on the second deck of the ferry. He watched a young girl and her father hold up potato chips, waiting for the seagulls to swoop down and take them from their hands. The weather wasn't as hot as in Alabama, but Robby had to wipe the sweat off his forehead. He thought about what he had agreed to do for a woman he barely knew. If one little thing went wrong, his actions could end with him sitting inside a jail cell.

"Let's go back to the truck. We will be docking in a few minutes," Sandra said, interrupting his thoughts.

Other than the color, almost every house looked exactly the same. Robby drove by the house twice before stopping at the curb across the street. Together, he and Sandra walked up and knocked on the door. Seconds later, a man in his late twenties or early thirties opened the door. As soon as he saw Sandra, he tried to close it. Robby pushed his way into the house, followed by Sandra.

He grabbed the man by the front of his shirt, backing him into the living room, then shoved him down in a chair. Sandra walked over, bent down, putting her face close to the man.

"Hello, Mark. I'll bet I'm the last person you expected to see at your door," she said.

"It wasn't me," Mark said.

"I know, but somehow you are involved in this. Where is he?" Sandra asked.

"I don't know who you are talking about," Mark said.

Taking that as his cue, Robby reached over and slapped Mark on the side of his head. Mark looked up. Robby saw the fear in the man's eyes.

"I'm not going to ask you again. Where is Dr. Hallmart?" he asked.

"I've already told you, I...." Mark stopped mid-sentence, looking past Robby.

"He lives next door!!" Mark yelled.

Robby turned around. His heart literally skipped a beat when he saw the gun in Sandra's hand. He started to protest, then realized her actions had worked.

"Put the gun away. There's no need for violence," came a voice from behind them.

Robby and Sandra both spun around. The man looked at least ninety years old. He held onto a cane to support his weight.

"May I sit down?" he asked. Sandra nodded toward a couch. After he was seated, she walked over and stood in front of him, then looked over at Robby.

"Mr. Robert Odell, meet Dr. David Hallmart," she said sarcastically. Both men nodded their heads.

"Why me?" Sandra asked.

"Because you refused to believe, and instead of just letting it go, you sent me that email calling me... I believe your words were... a crazy jerk," Dr. Hallmart said.

Sandra shook her head. "Why the games, and why did you wait over a year to give me a clue that would allow me to figure out who and where you were?" Sandra asked.

"I needed time to figure out where I went wrong and find a solution to the problem," Dr. Hallmart said.

"And the problem being?"

Dr. Hallmart laughed. "Look at us. We are both twenty-five years older than we should be. I tried the potion on myself. I thought it would take twenty-five years off my body, but instead, it had the opposite effect. Then I thought I had found the solution. I chose you for my experiment for two reasons. One, because you just happened to live in New York. And, two, I wanted to prove you wrong in thinking I was crazy. So when the potion had the same effect on you, I was heartbroken but also somewhat happy," he said.

Sandra sat down on the couch next to him. "Why were you happy?" she asked. Again, he laughed.

"Look at me, I'm sixty-three in a ninety-year-old body. If I had drunk the potion myself, it would have killed me. I did give you a choice, but I lied when I said it wouldn't work past midnight," he said.

Realizing she was still holding onto the gun, Sandra put it back inside her purse, then took out the first letter. "The morning I received this letter, I looked inside a window at the NBS news station. As it turns out, Mark, here, works for them. So, when you said you looked into my eyes, I thought maybe… Well, I really don't know what I thought, but figured it had something to do with all of this," Sandra said.

"I assure you that your thoughts and Mark working for NBS is pure coincidence, but now at this time, you are here. I believe I have figured out the solution, and I have a potion that should give us back our lost years. But, once again, you will have a choice. I will tell you I have tried it on animals, and it did work. This time, no games. The truth is if you drink it and it doesn't work, you could end up another twenty-five years older, which would make you between seventy-five and eighty years old. But if it does work, then you will have your youth back. Again, I say the choice is yours," Dr. Hallmart said.

"Where is this potion?" Sandra asked.

Dr. Hallmart looked past Sandra. "Mark will get it," he said. Robby and Sandra watched as Mark stood up and left the room.

"You will find what you seek next door," Robby said.

Sandra looked at him with a puzzled expression.

"The third part of the clue. We are next door to him," Robby said, pointing toward Dr. Hallmart.

Sandra stood up when she saw Mark walk back into the room. He was holding a small bottle containing a green liquid. He handed the bottle to Sandra. She walked over to Robby, reached inside her purse, took out the gun, and gave it to him.

"If I turn into an eighty-year-old woman, kill them both," she said, then removed the cap on the bottle and drank the liquid.

The room started spinning. She sat back down and closed her eyes. Three hours later, she opened her eyes. Robby, Dr. Hallmart, and Mark all stood looking down at her.

"Well?" she asked. Robby shook his head.

"It didn't work, but you're not any older," he said.

"Where is my gun?" she asked.

Dr. Hallmart took a step back. "Now, there's no need for that. I just need more time. I know I have come up with the right formula. I need to figure out in what order I should put it together," he said.

Robby helped Sandra to her feet. "We will give you one month. If you haven't figured it out by then, I will personally kill you," he said.

She was still wobbly on her feet, so Robby helped her out to the truck. A few minutes later, he parked on the ferry. "What now?" he asked.

"The hotel has a parking deck, so we go back there for the night, then we head back to Alabama tomorrow," Sandra said.

"But you're from New York, so why go back to Alabama?" Robby asked.

"Sandra laughed. "There is nothing here for me. Besides, I like it down south," she said.

***

The next morning, Robby was eating his breakfast when Sandra walked out of her bedroom. He stood up and smiled. "Well, young lady, are you going to call and let him know his new potion worked?" he asked.

Sandra smiled back at him. "Hell, no!" she said.

LUCY

CHAPTER 5

Joseph stood by the window, watching his wife and a young boy as they walked through the park across the street from the mental hospital where he had been a prisoner for the past five years. It was on this date every year that he would see them. This year, he wouldn't send one of the nurses out to speak with her, for he knew she would say she never knew him. Why did she say this? Who is the boy? How did this all start? Let's begin…

***

The old Culver ranch was no longer used for raising cattle; the previous owner died, leaving the ranch to his twenty-year-old granddaughter, Paula. Although she lived on the ranch all of her life, she didn't want the responsibility that came with it. She sold off most of the stock, let all of the ranch hands go, and would have sold the ranch if it hadn't been for the little white church.

As far back as she could remember, Paula had attended the little church her grandfather had built with his own hands. He preached his sermons every Sunday at noon. This gave the ranch hands time to finish their daily chores, gather their families, and report to the church. After the service, everyone sat at a long wooden table outside the church for their Sunday dinner.

It was at her grandfather's funeral that she met her husband. Joseph Cox had traveled all the way from Houston to Summerville for the purpose of preaching at her grandfather's funeral. From that day forward, he became the new pastor of the little white church and, one year later, Paula and he was married. It was on their wedding night that the angel gave them their quest.

***

One year after their marriage, Joseph Cox looked out over the congregation. It excited him to see the many people attending his service. He stepped up to the podium and began his message.

"Jesus Christ was a man, just like you and me. He walked the very same Earth we walk on today. He ate the same food, drank the same water, slept, wept, laughed, and died, just like everyone sitting inside this church has done and will do. Some of us may live to be over one hundred years old, and realistically, some of us may not live to see tomorrow. It is because our lives are so uncertain that I bring you this news: accept Jesus Christ as your Savior. I know some of you say you believe. My question to you is, do you truly believe? You can lie to me, lie to yourself, but you cannot, and I repeat, you cannot lie to God. He can read our thoughts. He wants us to stop our sinful ways and turn to him. I told you earlier, Jesus died, which is true. But now I will tell you that death could not hold Him, and He lives. Now, He sits at the right hand of God. And more good news, you can start right here today. God has instructed my wife and I to turn this ranch into a sanctuary for the believers. He wants all of us to live here as a community. I am asking you to join us. No one will force you to stay. You may come and go as you please. I asked you to do two things: Come down to this altar and ask God to forgive your sins. Then, go pack all of your belongings and return to the ranch."

Joseph stepped back and watched as the altar filled with people praying to God. As soon as one person would leave, another took their place. Once again, he looked out over the congregation. He saw his wife, Paula, standing at the back of the church. He didn't recognize the big man who stood behind her.

His mind went back to his youth. At age twelve, he decided to preach God's word. He had heard the evangelist, William Hammon, speak at a church near his home in Houston. It was that same day he bought his first Bible. Now, at age twenty-one, he had his own church.

***

Joseph sat on the steps of the new church. God had provided the necessary money needed to build it. Paula insisted on the new church being constructed beside the little white church that God had led him to a little over one year ago.

Joseph didn't hear anyone approach. When he lifted his head from prayer, a man sat beside him. "I'm sorry, I didn't hear you walk up. What can I do for you?" he asked. The man responded, "What you have in mind will work, but not at this time." Before Joseph could say anything, the man disappeared from his sight.

Paula walked up, holding two glasses of iced tea. She handed one of them to Joseph before she sat down beside him.

"Who were you talking to?" she asked.

"It was an angel," Joseph said without hesitation.

"What did he say?" Paula asked. Joseph reached over and kissed her on her cheek.

"He said everything was going to be okay," he said.

Paula stood up and looked down at Joseph. "I already know things are going to be okay. Now, tell me what he really said."

"He said our timing was off." Joseph looked at the ground between his feet. "I think this whole thing could blow up in our face," he said.

"What are you saying? Do you think this could turn out to be another Waco? We are not going to force anyone to stay here. You know yourself; we don't allow guns on this ranch. This is God's community. You and I were chosen by Him. Starting Monday, people will come from all over the county, bringing everything they own. Right now, at this time, you and I have to be strong. And I know in my heart, God will give us the strength to see this through," Paula said.

The two of them turned at the sound of a car approaching the church. The lights on the car's roof told them it was their friend, Sheriff Bill Williamson.

"Hi, Bill," Joseph said as the Sheriff stepped out of his car.

"What brings you all the way out here?" Paula asked.

"I really hate being the one who tells you this, but I'm afraid I have some bad news. There is a lot of negative talk going around town. People believe the two of you are starting some kind of convent. Some believe it may even be a cult of some sort. I just drove out here to get some facts," he said.

Paula spoke up. "Look, Bill, all we want to do is provide a place where people can hear the truth about Jesus and live their lives according to His plan for us. We are not doing anything wrong," she said.

Bill shook his head. He had known Paula all of her life and had been to the ranch a couple of times to hear Joseph preach. He liked both of them, but he had to keep the peace in his town.

"Did you know people are taking their money out of the bank?" Before either of them could answer, Bill continued, "Some of them are selling their land for little or nothing. Dammit, you two, they believe you are going to take the money and flee the country. Now, I'm not saying I believe any of this. I just wanted you to know what you're up against," he said.

"Listen, Sheriff. We are not planning on going anywhere. You can tell those townspeople that they are welcome to come out to this ranch at any time. All they will find here is the word of God being preached," Joseph said.

"We want to thank you for coming," Paula interjected. "But I want you to know that God is with us. It was He who gave us this plan a long time ago. As you can see, we are not breaking any laws, but if anything does happen, we will definitely give you a call."

***

Monday came and went without anyone coming to the ranch. Paula tried calling some of her closest friends. Not a single person answered. Tuesday morning, while Joseph was inside the little white church praying, Paula decided to drive into town. As she pulled her car out onto the highway, it wasn't long before she knew the problem. Some of the town men had used their trucks to block the road leading to the ranch. Paula knew she could trust God to protect her. Pulling her car over to the side of the road, she stepped out. Having no idea what to say, Paula trusted God to give her the words.

"What's going on?" she asked a tall man who was holding a double-barrel shotgun. If looks could kill, Paula knew she would already be dead. The man had eyes that told her he could be the devil himself. When the man didn't answer her question, she asked him again, "Can't you hear? I asked you what is going on here?"

"Look, lady. I don't know what you and the preacher husband are trying to pull, but let me tell you what I do know. My name is Jack Foster. My son and his wife tried to sell their house and everything else they owned. Said they were going to give the money to Jesus. Now, this takes us to something else I do know. You see, I read the book, and this Jesus feller died a long time ago, so there is no way he could be out at your ranch asking for their money. So, what you need to do is get back inside that pretty little car of yours and go back to where you came from, or I will do what I came out here to do in the first place," he said.

Paula raised her hands above her head. "God, in Jesus's name, I ask you to open the way for me to get to the town. In Your Word, You said all I had to do was ask, so please help me," she prayed. Seconds later, it looked like a tornado had blown across the road and flipped every truck on its side. The highway was now clear, and the men, not believing what they had witnessed, ran across a field in fear and disbelief. Paula knew the Angel of God had come through for her. She got back inside her car and drove on toward the town.

Paula knew who Jack was talking about; Ann and Ronald Foster were the first couple who committed to the church. They had heard

Joseph preach and decided they wanted to live more in the light of the truth. And, as it turned out, Ann became one of Paula's closest friends.

It was noon by the time Paula drove into the small town of Summerville, Texas. She couldn't believe what she saw. All the stores were closed. There wasn't a single person in sight. It was like the whole town had up and moved away. She drove to the end of Main Street before turning her car around. Halfway back through town, she saw a young boy standing in the middle of the street. She slammed on the brakes, sliding the car to a stop. The boy started running away from her. Realizing she had frightened him, Paula jumped out of the car. "Wait! I'm not going to hurt you. I just want to talk!" she yelled. The young boy stopped and turned around. He gave Paula a cold stare as she walked toward him. "Where is everyone?" she asked.

"They are having a meeting over at the school. The whole town is there." The young boy tilted his head. "Are you the devil?" he asked

. "No, I'm not the devil. Why do you ask such a question?" Paula said.

"My daddy said the devil lives out at the old ranch. Ain't you the lady who lives out there?" he asked.

"Yes, but I assure you, I'm not the devil. I come in the name of Jesus," she said.

The young boy shrugged his shoulders. "My daddy said they are going to run you and the preacher off of the ranch and burn down the church. It's what they are talking about now," he said. Paula walked back to her car.

"Well, we will just have to see about this, And, hey, thanks for telling me," she said.

The young boy had told the truth. The whole town was inside the school. Paula said a short prayer before getting out of her car. Every head in the auditorium turned as she walked through the door. Not one person spoke as she walked to the front of the crowd.

"I was just informed that you people are planning to burn our church." It was a statement more than a question as she looked out over the crowd. Everyone had their heads lowered. No one would look at her. At that moment, Jack Foster came running through the door. He stopped dead in his tracks when he saw Paula.

"Listen to me!" he yelled. "This woman is a witch. She just destroyed our trucks with her bare hands. She flipped them over like they were toys," he said. Several men came in behind Jack. All were nodding their heads to let the crowd know he was telling them the truth.

"No!" Paula cried out. "You people listen to me! Most of you in this room have known me all of my life. My grandfather has preached the Word of God for the past fifty years, and, as you know, he died a little over a year ago. I believe that he is in heaven right now looking down on us. It was when he died, God sent my husband to continue his work, and some of you have heard him preach and know he tells only the truth. Some of you would like to come live with us out at the ranch. Don't let these people stand in your way. Others say we want your money. So, here is what I want you to do. Donate your money to this school or a hospital or anywhere else you would like, then come out to the ranch. I promise you; God will take care of our needs."

No one said a word as Paula walked out of the school. Frank Foster made his way to the front. Everyone started talking at once.

"Quiet, everyone. Please, calm down and listen for a minute," Frank said. The noise subsided as everyone turned to look at him. "I know this sounds crazy, but some of us have just witnessed something that I swear don't make sense to us. Those trucks didn't flip themselves over. Believe me, when I say, it has to be some kind of evil force out there. We should stick to our plan. Let's go out there and burn that church to the ground," he said.

"Who died and left you in charge?" someone yelled from the back. "Yeah, we don't need you telling us what to do," someone else yelled out from the back. "Yeah, we don't need you telling us what to do," someone else echoed.

Ann Foster got up from her seat, walked over, and stood beside her father-in-law. She raised her hand, motioning for everyone to get quiet. "It's like Paula Cox said, most of you have heard her husband preach, and not one of you can say either of them have asked for your money.

As you know, they believe in their hearts that the end times are near. All they want to do is save your souls from hell. Yes, my husband and I are going out to the ranch with the sole purpose of stopping anyone who tries to harm those people." Ann turned and looked at Frank. His mouth was open as if he wanted to speak, but he couldn't find the words. "And there is nothing you, or anyone else, can do to stop us," she said.

Frank watched as the crowd walked out of the auditorium. "Mark my word. You will all be sorry!" he yelled.

***

Not long after Paula returned to the ranch, people started arriving. Ann Foster, along with her husband, Ronald, were the first. She told Paula she convinced some people to come and hear Joseph preach. One hour later, Joseph walked up to the podium. All of the pews were full. Some people stood in the aisles, and all eyes were on him.

"Let us pray, God, we are gathered together in the name of Your Son, Jesus. We believe he lived and died for us. We believe he will come again. Let us all be ready. Amen," he finished praying and continued addressing the crowd.

"I want to thank you all for coming. Some of you may find it hard to believe what I am going to say, but I give you my word; it's the honest truth. Several times, Paula and I have spoken to some of God's angels. The ones of you who have been out here and heard me preach, you know that all of my sermons have been based on the end times. I tell you, tonight, those end times are here. I have placed a notebook at the back. If you are willing to give your all to Jesus and come live with us here at the ranch, then sign your name and give the date you plan to come. Again, I thank you all for coming out tonight."

Three weeks later, a total of one hundred people lived on the ranch. Not a cross word was ever spoken by anyone. No one got sick or died. Like magic, a new box of food appeared inside the house every day. When asked where the food came from, Joseph told the story of Jesus feeding the thousands with the two fish and a few loaves of bread, and he knew God had supplied the food for them in the same way. Everything seemed perfect until the men came.

It was Sunday morning. All but a few people were inside the church. Out of nowhere, three men appeared in front of them. One of the men stepped forward and began to speak. "We have come from the Most High God with news of your future. Some of you have twenty-four hours to live here on Earth. Some of you have less. The end is at hand, so it's up to you what you do with this time. Now, go and sin no more." Before anyone could speak, the three men disappeared.

The church was silent until one of the women yelled out. "I don't want to die!" she said. Seconds later, there was total destruction. People ran over one another, trying to get out of the church. Six people died. Twenty minutes later, the only remaining people were Joseph, Paula, Ann Foster, and those six people. Joseph worked into the night, burying the dead while Paula and Ann stayed on their knees, praying God would send one of the angels to explain why this had happened.

Two days later, Joseph, Paula, and Ann sat on the church steps. The Angel they had been praying for appeared before them. He looked at Joseph. "I warned you the timing was wrong. You did not listen. I tell you now the time has come for you to complete the plan." Without saying anything else, the Angel disappeared. Joseph believed he knew what to do. The Rapture had come. The unbelievers were left behind. God had chosen him and Paula to convince them that Jesus would come back for those who came to believe.

***

Frank Foster sat inside his new truck. He found the truck sitting at a red light with the engine running. There was no one inside, so Frank took it upon himself to drive it away. Two blocks later, he picked up his passenger. The man was over six feet tall and weighed more than three hundred pounds.

"What did you say your name was?" Frank asked.

The big man looked over at him. "They call me Lucy," he said

"And what was it you want me to do?" Frank asked.

"I want you to go out to the Culver ranch and help the preacher get as many people as he can to move there," Lucy said.

"How will I convince him to trust me?" Frank asked.

"Tell him you have seen the same light as he, and you are willing to help. He will believe you," Lucy said. A flash of lightning blinded Frank. By the time he regained his sight, the big man was gone.

Frank was almost to the ranch when he saw the woman standing in the middle of the highway. He pulled the truck to a complete stop. The woman opened the door and climbed in. Frank couldn't stop himself from staring at her. The dress she wore barely covered her hips. Her breasts seemed too large for a woman her size.

"Where are you going, honey?"

She turned her body toward him, allowing the parting of her legs, which was the undoing of Frank. "Anywhere you are," she said with a smile. Frank looked up and down the highway. He wanted to be sure no one else was coming.

"I think you and I are going to get along just fine."

The woman slid across the seat, and Frank didn't notice the tiny sharp rod she held in her hand. He didn't notice her small hand moving toward his chest. He didn't feel anything as she pushed the rod through his heart. He didn't know when she grabbed the back of his head and covered his mouth with her own. He never felt when his soul left his body and entered the woman. "Don't we have somewhere to be?" she asked. Frank opened his eyes.

"Yes, I believe we do."

***

Ann sat on the porch of the ranch house. She looked up when she heard the truck as it stopped in front of her. She walked down the steps as Frank stepped out of the truck. "Hi, Baby!" He said with a smile. Ann hadn't seen Frank smile that way since the day she married his son. "What do you want, Frank?" she asked. "I came to talk to the preacher.

I have had a change of heart about a lot of things, and I want to help." Ann didn't know if she should believe him but decided to give him the benefit of the doubt. She reached over and kissed him on his cheek. It was then the woman stepped out of the truck. "Ann, this is Robin. She wants to join us," Frank said.

Joseph and Paula came out of the house, and introductions were made. The three women went inside the house. Joseph invited Frank to the church. When they sat on the front pew, Frank was the first to speak.

"I came to tell you, I have seen the same light you have, and I am here to help in any way I can," he said.

Joseph looked over at him. "The truth is, Frank, I am still trying to figure out how to go about doing what it is I need to do. But, thank you, and yes, I will accept your help. Now tell me, how bad is it out there?" he asked.

"Real bad. Most of the townspeople are gone. The ones who are left run around like mad dogs," Frank said.

Joseph stood up. "Let's go up to the house and get ourselves something to eat, and then I want you to drive me into town," he said.

"Okay, but let me be the first to tell you. You are not going to believe what you see," Frank said.

***

As soon as Joseph and Frank left for town, Paula decided to take a nap. She lay down across her bed. Ann asked Robin if she would like to take a look around the ranch. Robin accepted the offer for a tour. The two women walked for half an hour. They stopped for a moment to look inside both churches, then strolled past the barn where a few horses they had kept were housed. Finally, they ended up inside one of the bunkhouses. Several bunks lined each wall. Ann sat down on one of the bunks and leaned over, covering her face with her hands. Robin sat down next to her. She put her arm around Ann's shoulders. Suddenly, Ann felt an odd sensation throughout her entire body. She saw the tiny sharp rod in Robin's hand and watched Robin move closer. Ann's eyes fluttered closed, and she felt no pain as the sharp rod entered her heart and darkness came. When she opened her eyes, the two of them lay naked across the bunk. "Now, you are one of us."

***

Frank drove through the small town of Summerville, Texas. Joseph asked him to stop at the church. *If anyone had come to believe, they would be inside the church,* he thought to himself. Frank pulled the truck over to the curb. He saw Lucy standing across the street. "You go on inside. I have to go talk to someone," he said. Joseph opened the door and stepped out. "Okay. I'll meet you back here in a few minutes," he said.

Lucy led Frank down the street and behind the old post office. He had served his purpose; now, it was time to eliminate him. Frank's soul was already in hell, so he had no fear when the two creatures approached him. He felt no pain as they tore his body apart. Lucy let out a laugh, which sounded more like the roar of a lion. He had waited many years for this day.

Frank was nowhere in sight when Joseph came out of the church. He drove Frank's truck through town, looking for him. Frank had told the truth. Most of the townspeople were gone. The ones inside the church were trying to figure out a logical explanation as to what had happened. A few believed Jesus had taken the people who were saved. None wanted to return to the ranch with him.

He drove down every street looking for Frank. The sky above him turned black with clouds. Even though he felt guilty, Joseph decided to head back to the ranch before the storm hit. A mile out of town, Joseph saw something in the middle of the highway. He slid the truck to a stop. Joseph thought someone had placed a towel over a ball at first sight, but he felt sick to his stomach when he removed the towel. Frank's eyes looked up at him from his decapitated head. A note written in bold letters had been taped to it.

SHE WILL BE MINE.
LUCY FURR

Joseph rewrapped Frank's head in the towel, then lay it on the truck seat beside him. He drove on toward the ranch. The sky became darker. He stepped down on the gas pedal, forcing the truck to move faster. He could barely see in front of him. He should have reached the road leading out to the ranch some time ago. *There was no way he could have missed it,* he thought. He saw the blue lights of a Texas State Trooper car flashing in his rearview mirror. "Thank God!" he said aloud.

***

Paula awoke to find herself tied to the big four-poster bed. She had some sort of blindfold tied around her head. "Is anyone here?" she yelled. No one answered. "God, please help me," she said.

"I am here, child." A voice spoke to her. Lucy reached out and removed the blindfold. It took Paula's eyes a few seconds to adjust to the light. She saw the big man standing beside her bed. "Who are you?" she shouted.

"I'm the god you have been praying to all these years," he said.

"No, I pray only to Jesus," Paula said. It was then she realized she lay naked in front of him. "What are you going to do to me?" she cried. Lucy let out a laugh.

"It's already done, child, and now I will tell you why. Many years ago, I watched as you were born. It was at your birth that you were given to me by your grandfather. He couldn't meet the mortgage, and the people at the bank planned to take the ranch away from him. The god he was praying to wouldn't help, so he turned to me. I gave him everything he wanted and, in return, he gave me you. Now the time has come for you to bear my son, for he will rule this world."

THE BIG STORM

CHAPTER 6

My name is Oscar Vann. My infatuation with storms is why I am where I am today. The first time I saw lightning strike, I was six years old. I lived on a farm with my grandparents. My grandfather said I was crazy. It didn't matter if it was day or night. Every time a storm came up, I ran to our barn, climbed up into the loft, opened the hay doors, and sat with my legs hanging over the barn loft entrance. During my freshman year of high school, I started studying weather patterns and decided to become a meteorologist.

I graduated with a Bachelor's degree in Science from Auburn University and got a job working at a local TV station near my home in Dothan, Alabama. On my twenty-fifth birthday, I received news that I thought was the best birthday present I could ever get. Five big storms were coming from five different directions. A group of meteorologists were to board a plane in Venezuela and fly above the storms. If all five storms met together, it could be the biggest storm ever recorded, and I had been chosen to be one of the meteorologists.

The plan was for me to fly from Miami to San Juan, Puerto Rico. I would then fly to Venezuela, meet the others, and board the plane that would fly us above the storms. I never boarded that plane.

It was somewhere between San Juan and Venezuela that one of the storms changed direction. The plane I was on flew directly into it. I had a window seat. I remember seeing lightning strike the wing. I saw the engine blow up, then something hit me above my right eye. The next thing I remember is the taste of saltwater in my mouth. A wave rolled over me. When the water receded, I was face down on the sand. I crawled further up onto the beach. My head hurt, I couldn't see out of my right eye, and the rain came down so hard that I could barely see anything out of my left one. I rolled over onto my back. Lightning lit up the sky. I took the opportunity to look up and down the beach. I thought I saw someone coming toward me, but I wasn't sure. I jumped to my feet when I heard the sound of someone screaming to my left, then someone else on my right. The sound on my right seemed closer, so I ran toward it. I found a woman lying half in and half out of the water. I helped her to her feet. She tried to talk, but I couldn't understand a word she said with the rain and wind. I led her up onto the beach and set her beside a palm tree. I told her to wait and that I would come back for her.

I walked closer to the water as the night was pitch-black. I waited for another lightning strike to see further down the beach. I saw someone. I ran to where I thought they should be and yelled as loud as I could. The lightning strikes were getting further apart, but the sky brightened again, and I saw two children not far from where I stood. I walked over to where they sat. A young boy was crying out for his mother; the young girl stood up but didn't say anything. I picked the boy up, grabbed the girl's hand, and led them to where I had left the other woman.

I don't know why I was doing what I was doing, but in my mind, I had to see if I could help anyone else, so I ran back down the beach. I saw what I thought was another child crawling toward the water. It turned out to be a young woman with both her legs amputated above her knees. I thought, at first, she had lost her legs during the crash, but as it turned out, she had lost them years earlier. I dropped down on my knees beside her. With lightning speed, she flipped over on her back and took a swing at me. I grabbed both of her hands and pinned her arms to the sand. I assured her I only wanted to help. She started crying. I picked her up and carried her to where I had left the others. Once again, I ran down the beach. The rain had stopped, and there was no more lightning. I felt the pain in my head. I could barely see. I tripped and fell headfirst into the sand. I realized I had tripped over a woman. I crawled back to where she lay. Her body seemed ice cold. I realized she was dead. I rolled over on my back and closed my eyes. I don't know how long I had laid there when I felt the sun on my face. I opened my left eye. I reached up and touched my right eye. It was swollen shut with a big knot above it.

I sat up and looked around. I could see five bodies. Three men and two women. I touched each one to be sure that they were dead. Both women wore dresses with no pockets. I searched the men and found two cell phones and a cigarette lighter. The phones didn't work, so I put them back inside their pockets. I kept the lighter. I drug the bodies up into the tree line, then walked back to where I had left the others.

This was my first good look at them; they were all asleep. The woman had long blond hair. She wasn't what I would call fat, but she was big-boned. The boy had jet black hair and dark skin. I guessed him to be around nine or ten years old. The young girl also had blond hair. She wore a tee shirt and a pair of blue jean shorts. She had long skinny legs. I guessed her age at eleven or twelve. As it turned out, I was right on both counts. The boy was ten, and the girl was twelve. I looked at the woman with no legs. She had short reddish hair. Her face wasn't what I would call pretty, but she also wasn't ugly. Back home, we would have called her plain Jane or homely. She was the first to wake. She looked up at me, blinked her eyes several times, then rolled over on her back and sat up. She asked if I had found her sister. I didn't tell her about the dead bodies. Instead, I told her I had been several miles in both directions, and as far as I knew, the five of us were the only ones who survived the crash. She covered her face with her hands and cried.

The big-boned woman, boy, and girl all awoke at the same time. The big-boned woman asked me if I was okay. She crawled over, reached out, and touched my right eye. I realized why I couldn't understand what she was saying when I found her; the woman had Down syndrome. I asked her name. She said it was Martha and that she was on her way to visit her aunt and uncle in Maracaibo. I knew then that she really didn't understand the severity of our situation.

The boy started to cry again. I assured him we were going to be alright and someone would soon come for us. I asked him his name. He said it was Tim, and even though I didn't ask, he said he was ten years old. I looked at the young girl. When I asked her name, she didn't answer. She had the prettiest blue eyes I had ever seen. It was Martha who said she thought the girl was mute. This surprised me. I had always believed people with Downs Syndrome were what our society related to as retarded. It didn't take me long to figure out that I was an idiot. This woman was far from being retarded.

Martha stood up, reached down, took the girl's hand, and helped her to her feet. She then walked over and picked up the woman with no legs. She told me they were going into the bushes to relieve themselves. It was then the woman with no legs turned to me. She said her name was Christine, but people called her Christy for short. It wasn't until she smiled that I realized she had made a joke. I told them my name and wished we had all met somewhere besides here.

When they came back, Martha held Christy on her side with one arm and cradled four coconuts in the other. The blue-eyed girl also carried both arms full of coconuts. Martha sat Christy down, took two of the coconuts, and banged them together. Both nuts cracked open. She saved as much of the milk as she could. She gave some of the milk to the boy, then some to the blue-eyed girl. She cracked open two more. She gave one to Christy, then tried to hand the other one to me. I shook my head and told her to drink it herself. I reached down and picked up two of the coconuts, banged them together, and when they didn't break, Martha laughed. She took them out of my hands, cracked them, and handed them back to me. I realize now that it was at that very moment, she won my heart.

We sat for a little while, looking out at the ocean. It was Christy who asked how long it would be before someone came for us. I told her by now, people would know the plane was down and should be coming soon. I guess it was out of boredom, and needing something to do with my hands, I took the cigarette lighter out of my pocket. I spun the wheel and watched a tiny flame appear.

When Martha saw it, she insisted we make a pile of palm leaves on the beach. When we saw a plane or ship, we could light a fire so they could see the smoke. I carried Christy out and sat her on the beach. Martha, Tim, the blue-eyed girl, and I made a pile of leaves higher than my head. Two days went by without a plane or ship appearing. It was Christy who told me that I should go look for other people. She said as far as we knew, there could be people who lived on the island. Tim wanted to go with me and cried when I told him no. I had to convince him that the woman would need a man to look out for them. I really wouldn't have minded the company, but I knew I would pass by those dead bodies, and I didn't want Tim to see them. Still, I waited until the next morning before I left.

As I approached the bodies, the smell of rotting flesh invaded my nose. I threw up what little I had left in my stomach, then ran down the beach, leaving the odor behind me. I walked for what seemed like hours. I looked up at the mountain; I don't know why I hadn't noticed it before. I guessed it to be no more than a couple of miles high and not too steep. I thought if I could climb to the top, I would be able to see how big an island we were on. It was then that I saw the plane or at least part of the aircraft. Half of it lay on the beach, the other half in the water. I ran toward it. I was about twenty-five yards away when I stopped dead in my tracks. Once again, the smell of rotting flesh invaded my nose. I realized this wasn't the plane we were on but the middle section of a military aircraft.

I knew it wasn't from the United States when I saw the flag painted on the side. I knew I had seen the flag before, but I couldn't remember what country it represented. I took off my shirt, wrapped it around my face as I climbed up onto the plane. I saw two dead bodies, one man and one woman, both wearing military uniforms. I counted six pallets covered with green tarps. The dead man had a twelve-inch knife with a compass on the handle strapped to his side. I used the knife to cut the ropes that held the green tarps closed.

I couldn't believe my luck. I had a friend back home who did a two-year bid in the Army. He brought some boxes to my house. He called them MREs—Meals Ready to Eat. Although the writing on these boxes was different, I know I was looking at a whole pallet of food. I cut the ropes off the other five pallets. Three more were food, one pallet held bottled water, and once again, I couldn't believe my luck. The last tarp I pulled away was a whole pallet of beer. I took a can of beer, pulled the tab, and drank it down without removing the can from my mouth. I opened several boxes of MREs, eating only meat. I poured the remaining contents of several boxes onto the floor. Besides the packets of meat, there were crackers and peanut butter. Another container had some kind of soup, a book of matches, and paper towels that were supposed to double as toilet paper.

I looked around the plane; several wooden boxes were lining one wall. The tops were nailed shut, so I picked up one of the boxes, raised it above my head, then dropped it on the floor of the plane. The box came apart. Inside were several medal sprockets of various sizes, each one coated in some kind of wax. I rolled the two dead bodies out of the plane, then dragged them into the trees. Once back inside the plane, I found a military backpack made of the same material as the tarps. I realized that by opening the food boxes and then dumping them into the pack, I could carry more food. So I filled the backpack to the top with food, water, and a six-pack of beer for myself, then headed back to where I had left the others.

Several hours later, I saw Tim running toward me. I knelt down on one knee and waited for him. I told him to reach inside the pack and get himself a bottle of water. He tried to drink it all down, but I stopped him. I told him to take small sips to keep from making himself sick. He told me the women were okay; he had watched out for them. I stood up, patted him on top of his head, and told him he did well.

Martha helped me remove the backpack. She took out bottles of water. She made sure everyone else had water before she drank any herself. I thought back to the coconuts. She wouldn't eat until she was sure everyone else had eaten. It was then she won my heart, but now I had fallen in love with her. Not romantically, but more like a sister.

I told them about the plane and what I found inside. At first, I left out the details of the two dead bodies, then I decided to tell them about those two and the five I had found on the first day.

The sun was going down, so we decided to wait until the next day before we went to the plane. Christy told me she wanted to see the two dead women. She said she had to know if one of those women was her sister. I guess I was tired from the day's walk, and I assumed the beers I'd drank could have helped with my drowsiness. As soon as I lay down, I went to sleep. When I woke up, it was morning. The others were all down on the beach waiting for me. Once again, Martha surprised me with her wit. She took the backpack and, using the knife, put two holes in the bottom, leaving a strip in the middle. She slipped the pack over Christy's stumps, then slit the sides to allow for her arms. I remembered seeing women carrying babies in something like this, but I knew I wouldn't have thought of creating one for Christy.

I helped Martha strap the pack to herself and helped her to her feet. She stumbled a little at first, then managed to keep her balance. I asked her if she wanted me to carry Christy. She said she could handle it, but still, I held on to her arm as we walked down the beach.

It took us forty-five minutes to reach the place where I dragged the dead bodies to the tree line. I guided everyone down next to the water, trying to avoid the odor. I took off my shirt, handed it to Christy, and told her to wrap it around her nose. She said she didn't know which would be worse, the dead bodies or my shirt. It wasn't until she smiled that I realized she had made another joke.

I helped Martha sit Christy down, then Martha helped me strap her to my back. We were almost to the bodies when I heard Martha yell my name. When I managed to turn around, the blue-eyed girl stood beside me. I guess it was from the look in her eyes that I could tell she, too, was looking for someone. I reached down, took her hand, and walked on toward the trees. When we reached the bodies, she looked up, shook her head, let go of my hand, and ran back toward Martha. The bodies themselves were unrecognizable. Christy said she could tell by the clothes they wore that neither of them was her sister.

We walked on toward the plane. Martha and I took turns carrying Christy. Tim stayed a hundred yards or so ahead of us. I saw him take off running when the plane came into sight. I saw him climb up into the plane, then jump back down. He ran back toward us. I smiled when I saw what he carried. He had three bottles of water and one can of beer. He handed the two women and the blue-eyed girl a bottle of water; he gave me the can of beer. In truth, I would rather have had the water, but I drank the beer to keep from hurting his feelings. I noticed the water level inside the plane had risen at least three feet. I knew this meant one of two things: the plane was either sinking down into the sand or sliding out into the ocean.

We started unloading the plane. We carried some of the food up next to the trees, then realized we could still smell the dead bodies, so we moved further down the beach. Before we had unloaded a whole pallet of food, it started raining. Martha and I helped Christy up onto the plane. Then I helped Martha climb up. She threw down one of the tarps. Tim and I carried it down the beach and covered the boxes of food before we climbed back inside the plane.

It rained the rest of that day and most of the night. Sometime before morning, I had fallen asleep, and when I woke up, it had stopped raining, and everyone was outside. When I jumped down from the plane, I saw Christy and the blue-eyed girl sitting next to the food boxes. I saw Martha and Tim further down the beach. They were running back towards us, waving their arms over their heads. At first, I thought they were saying they had found Dave. It wasn't until they reached us and caught their breath that Tim told me they had found a cave. He said there was a waterfall and a pool of freshwater. He said it would be a good place for us to live while we were on the island. I knew I had hurt his feelings when I told him we didn't need a cave to live in because I was sure someone would come to rescue us. Without saying a word, he looked up at me then walked down toward the water. Martha told me that she, too, believed someone would come for us, but she also thought the cave would be a better place for us to live until they did. So, I walked down to the water and told Tim I wanted him to show me the cave.

One week later, we finally had carried all the food, water, and beer to the cave, which, in itself, wasn't very big. It was about ten feet wide and no more than twenty feet deep. The opening was small at three feet wide and only five feet tall, but once inside, the ceiling was at least fifteen feet above our heads. The waterfall consisted of a four-foot-wide stream of water running down the mountain and falling into a twenty-foot shallow pool. It wasn't big enough to swim in, but at least we could take a fresh bath, and the water was suitable for drinking.

We were on an uphill grade about fifty yards up into the trees, but I could still see the ocean and sky if a ship or plane came by.

Once again, Martha insisted we make a pile of palm leaves on the beach. Tim and I did this while the women worked on other tasks. Upon her inspection of our living arrangement, Christy discovered the sprockets from the plane that were covered in wax. She came up with the idea of making candles. She had Martha built a fire and cut the tops out of several beer cans. Christy stripped the wax from the sprockets then packed as much as possible into the beer cans. She sat the cans next to the fire until the wax melted, then she moved the cans away from the fire and put some kind of string down inside them. Christy worked all that day, and when she finished, we had twenty new candles. We had to burn three at a time inside the cave to give us enough light.

Martha and the blue-eyed girl cut strips from one of the green tarps, then they cut some of the others in half. They folded the half tarps, sewed them together, then stuffed the ends with palm leaves, making each of us a mattress to sleep on. I could see we had all fallen into a daily routine of trying to make our new home as comfortable as possible. It was like we all hoped to go home, but none of us believed we ever would.

One day out of the blue, I decided I would climb the mountain. I wanted to be sure we were alone or that we were even on an island. I decided to take the blue-eyed girl with me. Once again, Tim got angry and pitched a fit. Once again, I had to convince him I needed a man to say with the women, and he fell for it. All this time, I never noticed the blue-eyed girl wore no shoes, and it was when I saw Martha tying her own shoes on the girl's feet, I wished my own shoes could have been softer. But my old penny loafers would have to do.

The uphill climb wasn't as bad as I thought it would be. We made good time on the first day. By dark, we were more than halfway up the mountain. However, on the second day, we encountered a few hiccups. We came upon some boulders that we couldn't climb, so we backtracked to go around them. It was in one of the trips around a giant boulder when we found the birds. There were hundreds of them. I didn't know what kind they were. They had blue-gray feathers and short fat wings, which actually prevented them from flying. They were smaller than a turkey and bigger than a chicken. This didn't really matter because what I saw in my mind was one of these birds with its feathers plucked, roasting over an open fire. I picked up a baseball-sized rock. I figured if I threw it amongst the birds, I would hit at least one, and if I didn't kill it, maybe it would be crippled enough for me to catch it. But before I had time to rear back my arm, the blue-eyed girl ran in amongst them herself. When she walked back to where I stood, she had one of the birds in each of her hands.

We backtracked until we found the stream of water running down the mountain. Even though there were several hours of daylight left in the day, we set up camp. I tried plucking one of the birds but wasn't doing too good a job, so I decided to skin it instead. By the time I finished, the blue-eyed girl had gathered wood and built a fire. I rigged a skewer and two forked sticks. Then, together, we sat watching the birds cook. The sizzling sound of the fat grease dripping into the fire was music to my ears. I told the blue-eyed girl how I had grown up on a farm. How we used to kill our own chickens and hogs. I still don't know if she understood a single word I said. Every now and again, she would look up at me and nod her head.

Together, we finished off one of the big birds. We didn't have anything to wrap the other bird in, so we stuck it down inside our makeshift pack with our other supplies.

There were still a couple of hours of daylight left, so we decided to keep going. It was dusk when we reached the top of the mountain. I was right. I could see all the way around the island, but it was too dark for me to tell if anyone else was down there. I built a fire, reheated the bird, and ate some of it. The blue-eyed girl ate peanut butter and crackers out of the MRE boxes. The weather seemed cooler than it did down below, so I stacked more wood on the fire before we went to sleep. The following day when I woke up, the blue-eyed girl was standing by a cliff looking down the mountain. When I walked up beside her, she pointed out toward the ocean. I saw the ship. I could also see smoke coming from a fire down on the beach. I knew then that Martha, Christy, and Tim had also seen it. I started laughing. I jumped up and down. I picked up the blue-eyed girl and spun her around in a circle. When I put her down, I saw tears running down her face. At first, I thought they were tears of joy, then she shook her head and pointed back toward the ship. It was then I realized that the ship had gotten smaller. No one had seen the fire. It was the first time since we crashed on the island that tears ran down my own face.

I took another look around the island. I didn't see any sign of anyone else, so we packed up and started back down. I guess it was because we knew the route that we made a better time going down. The birds were in the exact spot as before. The blue-eyed caught and killed four of them. When we made it back to the stream, I gutted them out but left the feathers on them. I built a fire and cooked the gizzards and livers. At first, the blue-eyed girl refused the offer of the liver, but when she saw me eat one, she held out her hand. It turned out that she ate three of the four.

We stopped again at dark. I knew if we kept going, we could be at the cave in a couple of hours, but I didn't want to take the chance of stumbling over something and getting hurt. In the morning, I let the blue-eyed girl sleep while I finished cleaning the four birds. Two and a half hours later, we were back at the cave.

Martha, Christy, and Tim all tried talking simultaneously, each telling their version of the ship. I told them we had also seen the ship and how we had cried. Christy patted herself and then pointed toward Martha. She said we weren't the only ones who cried. I told them we had something which should cheer them up. I dumped the four birds on the ground. Martha washed them in the pool while Tim and I built a fire. That day we all ate our fill.

A few days later, Tim and I were down on the beach catching sand crabs for our dinner. I saw a dark cloud roll out over the ocean. When I realized it was coming toward us, I threw down the crabs, grabbed Tim's hand, and ran back toward the cave. I told Martha we needed to put everything we owned inside. I told all of them if I was right; we had less than an hour before the storm hit. As it turned out, I was right. No sooner than we had everything inside and the door secure, the rains came along with the wind. I had built a door out of the wooden crate from the plane and propped it up with bamboo poles. The wind blew hard; the door shook but stayed in place. The thunder was loud and seemed to last forever. This went on for at least three hours, then everything got quiet. Christy asked if the storm was over. I told her no, the stillness was because we were in the eye of a hurricane, and the worst was yet to come. Once again, I was right. It wasn't long until the thunder rolled again, and the wind started back up. Four hours later, the wind died down. I opened the door enough for me to slip out. I looked out at the ocean. The waves were high. The white caps ended a few yards from the cave. I knew if that storm had been worse, we could have all drowned.

I sat on a boulder and watched the waves. Minute by minute, they grew smaller and smaller until I could see the sand on the beach. I walked down to where the plane was supposed to be. As I expected, it had been washed out into the ocean.

I guess it was because I thought we would never leave the island that I lost it. I sat down on the sand. When I came to my senses, I knew I had been sitting there for a while. In fact, I had been sitting there for so long that I didn't bother to get up to relieve myself. I sat in my soiled clothes for some time before the smell got to me. I looked around, but I was alone. I walked down the beach to where the freshwater stream ran into the ocean. I stripped naked, bathed myself, then washed out my clothes. I put my wet clothes on, then walked back to the cave.

Martha and Christy were sitting outside on the ground. Both looked up at me, but neither spoke. Martha stood up and walked inside the cave. A minute later, she came back out and handed me some food. I ate in silence for a few minutes, then Christy asked if I was back. I could tell she didn't just mean physically. I asked Christy if they knew what happened to me, shaking her head; no one knew. She said I sat on the beach staring at the ocean for four days, and I wouldn't talk to anyone. I assured her I was back and hoped I would never go there again.

I didn't see Tim nor the blue-eyed girl, so I asked Martha where they were. She said they went up the mountain. She said she tried to stop them, but Tim had it in his head that he was now the man and wouldn't listen to her. I told Martha she didn't have to worry. The blue-eyed girl knew the way and wouldn't let anything happen to Tim. It was no more than a few minutes later, the two of them came running toward us. The blue-eyed girl held up two of the big birds, but Tim seemed the most excited. He ran up to me, holding the knife. He reached out and unscrewed the compass revealing a hollow handle, which had some fishing line, two fish hooks, and two stick matches. It was that day Tim caught his first shark.

Twenty years have passed since the day we crashed on the island. A lot of things have happened. Tim fell and broke his leg. We set it the best we could, but he still walks with a limp to this day. Martha got sick and died. It broke all our hearts. We buried her next to the cave. Christy and I came together as a couple, so did Tim and the blue-eyed girl. Tim gave her a name. He called her Pebbles. Tim said that he got the name from a cartoon he watched when he was back home. She had a baby, and I delivered it myself. It was a boy; they named him Bam Bam.

It was Tim who saw the ship and lit the fire. At first, we thought no one had seen the smoke, then we saw the small powerboat coming toward us. Right now, I sit here watching Christy sleep in a real bed. Well, it's really a ship's bed. We are waiting on some men to come back with Martha's remains. I refused to leave the island without her. It was the captain of this ship who assured me he would send someone to bring her aboard.

I don't even know where we will go from here. I do know people will think I'm crazy, but the truth is, at this moment in time... I wish the damn ship had never come. I long to be back home on our island.

THE ACCIDENT

CHAPTER 7

Today started like most others, although my truck did begin on the first try. Usually, my old 1972 Ford would almost drain her battery before she started. I drove to the end of my street and turned right, facing the sun. A quarter-mile down, I always turned left so the sun would no longer be in my eyes. I knew I was close to the turn because my turn signal was already on. Suddenly, everything went dark like the sun was one big eye, and it had blinked. When the light came back, the street beneath my truck tires had turned to dirt. I slammed on my brakes, threw the gear shift into park, and jumped out of my truck. I started shaking my head from side to side and blinked my eyes repeatedly. The world, as I knew it, had changed. My left turn had disappeared. There wasn't another road in sight.

I heard the horses before I saw them. There were carrying twenty blue-uniformed soldiers with rifles. I turned to run. I heard a man's voice yell for me to stop. I did as he asked, but the whole time I found that I couldn't stop laughing. In my mind, I knew none of this could be real. I figured I was either asleep, dying, or this was a fever dream. I stopped laughing when I realized all twenty men had their rifles pointed at me. I believe it was the man yelling for me to stop who climbed off of his horse. "Are you Jason Pruitt?" he asked. My mind started turning over, running a hundred miles an hour. Again, I thought this had to be a dream of some kind, but I decided to go along with it.

"Who's asking?" I said.

"Sir, I'm Sergeant Hightower from the General's Union Army. My unit was sent from Washington to find you and carry what you have on your person back to the General," he said.

"To answer your question, yes, I am Jason Pruitt, but I have no idea what you are talking about. Hell, man, I don't know where I am or how I got here. And, hey, I'm gonna go out on a limb here and say that I really don't believe any of this is real."

It was then that the man who called himself Sergeant Hightower walked over and punched me in the stomach. It caused me to double over and fall to the ground. As soon as I could catch my breath, I jumped to my feet.

"What the hell did you do that for?" I asked.

"It was to show you this is real and that your life depends on what you have brought with you. So, I'll ask you kindly, sir. Give it to me, and we will be on our way," he said. I took a few steps back to put some distance between us.

"Look, man. I have already told you that I have no idea what you are talking about, but if you tell me what it's supposed to be and if I do have it- I promise it's yours."

Sergeant Hightower turned toward the other man. "Corporal!" he yelled. A short, stocky man climbed down off of his horse and ran to us. The corporal reached inside his coat pocket and brought out a piece of paper. He handed it to Hightower, who then gave it to me.

"This should explain everything," he said.

"I think we could have gotten off to a better start if you had given me this letter earlier," I said sarcastically.

Hightower looked at me, then shrugged his shoulders. I unfolded the piece of paper and read its contents.

Jason, if you are reading this letter, then my plan has worked. I know this is probably blowing your mind, but you need to trust me. You are standing in the year 1857. Now, once you wrap your head around this, take a deep breath because there is more... You see, you and I haven't met yet, but we will about five or so years in your future. Together, along with your wife, Karen, who you also haven't yet met, invented a machine that allows us to travel back in time. I discovered we could send anyone from any time zone to any place we wanted, which is why you are where you are. Come with these men and bring your truck. I will explain more once you arrive.

Your future friend,
Mallory Galson

Again, my mind was racing. I turned back toward Hightower.

"How far is it from here to Washington?" I asked.

"Two days ride from here," he said.

Calculating the distance in my head, the horses could travel at least thirty miles a day, so he was talking about sixty miles, more or less. I looked at the condition of the road. If it was like this the entire distance, I could be there in three hours or less. I looked back up at Hightower.

"Have you read this letter?"

Hightower looked down at the ground. "No, sir. I can't read."

I still wasn't sure of the reality of the situation but decided to go along. "Okay, Sergeant. From now on, you take orders from me." I pointed, and Hightower glanced in the direction of where my finger led. He looked at the truck curiously.

"This is what your General wants; so, you and I will carry it to him."

Hightower looked at the truck and then back at me. "Where are your horses?"

I walked over and raised the hood on my truck.

"I have three hundred fifty-one of them inside this thing called an engine." Hightower laughed, looking closely under the hood. "They must be mighty small horses; I don't know how they gonna go faster than them horses." Hightower looked over at the men on horses and smiled as he glanced at me.

Shaking my head while dismissing his words, I walked over and opened the passenger door. "Tell your men to move out of my way. Climb inside here, and I will show you how one of my horses is faster than all of yours put together."

Hightower hesitated for a moment, but being a man conditioned to following orders, he complied.

"Get those horses off the road!" he yelled before climbing into the truck. I got behind the wheel, thankful it started on the first try.

I looked over at Hightower and smiled. "Hold on!" Hightower looked at me cautiously and then looked at my arm. Dismissing some internal thought, he found the rest on the side of the door and grabbed it.

I placed the gear shift in drive as I pressed the gas pedal to the floor. The back tires spun, slinging dirt and rocks all over the other men. Hightower let go of the door rest and gripped the dashboard with both hands bracing himself. He looked at me but didn't say a word as we raced down the narrow road. I looked at the speedometer. We were only going forty-five miles per hour, but I knew, to Hightower, it must have seemed like we were traveling at the speed of light. It wasn't long until I had to slow down. The road had places where the rain had washed the road path away. My truck walked over the ruts at a crawl, but once we were back on solid ground, I stomped down on the gas. At one point, I had my truck going over seventy miles per hour.

Hightower still hadn't said a word. The road started an uphill grade, then down, and around a sharp curve. I was traveling too fast and missed the turn. We ended up stopping in the middle of a field. Before I realized what was happening, my truck was surrounded by soldiers in gray uniforms. Once again, I stepped down on the gas pedal. I spun the truck around in a circle, knocking most of the soldiers to the ground. I heard several shots fired, but not one bullet hit my vehicle.

Once we were back on the road and the soldiers were out of sight, Hightower spoke.

"Are you and this here contraption from our world?" he asked. I stopped the truck, thought for a moment, then looked at him.

"Remember how you convinced me that this is real?"

He looked at me and said Yeah.

I reached back with my hand and made a fist, and punched him in the nose; he instinctively covered his face with his hands. Shaking off the pain, he started laughing as he turned and looked at me.

"Yeah, I guess you owed me that one," he said as he wiped a trickle of blood with his sleeve from his nose. He looked out the window at what was around us, then inspecting the truck; I watched him cautiously.

He turned his attention to me with a searching look.

"Can you tell me what in tarnation I have gotten myself into?" he asked.

I put the truck in gear and slowly moved on. "It's like I said when we first met- I don't know what's going on here. However, according to the letter you gave me, and I don't expect you to understand any of this, but your General and I met one another in the year 2025. We created a machine that allows people to travel through time. Now, here is the kicker in all of this. I came here from the year 2015 before the machine was created, so I'm as much in the dark here as you are." Hightower nodded his head.

We traveled in silence as I observed the landscape changing. "Do you know how far it is to Washington from here?" I asked.

He looked out the side window, then turned and looked behind us.

"Yeah, it's not too far, and in this contraption, we should be there in a matter of minutes."

As soon as I saw the fort, I stopped the truck. "Welcome to Washington," Hightower said. It was my turn to laugh. In my mind, I pictured concrete buildings and paved streets, but here I sat, looking at a fort built out of chopped-down pine trees.

"Why are you stopping? Hightower asked.

Looking at Hightower, I considered what I was getting myself into, so I asked, "How many are inside the fort?"

Acknowledging my thoughts, Hightower answered my questions without hesitation.

"Six, besides the General, and that nut case he has locked up inside the stockade. The rest of the men won't be back until sometime tomorrow," he said.

"Who is the nutcase?" I asked.

"Some woman. Her name is Karen. She keeps saying she is from the future-" Hightower stopped mid-sentence. He reached up with one hand scratching his head.

"You know, now that I think of it, the woman might not be as crazy as the General said." He said, finishing his thought.

"What makes you say this?" I ask

"Hell, look at me. I'm sitting inside something which can move across the ground faster than lightning, which you say comes from the future. So, I'm looking at it this way... I must be as crazy as she is, or she isn't crazy at all."

"I'm guessing the latter," I said.

I drove toward the fort going ten miles an hour. The gate swung open. A short, stocky man stepped out and pointed his rifle towards us. I reached over Hightower, pulled the door handle, and pushed it open.

"Get out. Tell him who you are." Hightower stepped out of the truck.

"Put that thing down, Sid. It's me. Move aside, we are coming in." Sid, looking at the truck, followed Hightower's command.

Assessing my surroundings after getting out of the truck, I guessed the fort to be fifty square yards with four buildings inside. I looked over at Hightower. "Which one of these buildings is the stockade?"

Hightower pointed toward the smallest of the four buildings. I walked over, hesitated for a moment, then opened the door and stepped inside. A woman with fiery red hair sat on an iron bunk; one of her legs had been shackled and chained to it. As soon as she saw me, tears ran down her face.

"Do you know who I am?" I asked softly

She nodded her head. "Don't you know I am going to get you out of here?" I asked.

She shook her head from side to side. "He's crazy. He won't let you. I heard him tell the men he sent as soon as they got what he needed; they were to kill you."

"Don't listen to her, Jason."

I spun around at the sound of his voice. The man standing there was taller than me, but I outweighed him by at least forty pounds. I reached out, grabbed him by his shirt, and slammed him against the wall. I felt a pain in the back of my head. Before my lights went out, I turned in time to see Hightower standing behind me.

When I woke up, the man sat in a chair across from me. We stared at one another for a few minutes. Realizing I wasn't tied up or chained, I stood up.

"Before you go crazy on me again, I must tell you, in the future, you and I are best friends. We both work for a company named NIFS— Natural Institute of Future Science. The company produces magnetic fields that help aircraft travel into outer space. The company was under investigation on three different occasions when an aircraft passed through the ozone and disappeared. It was you who figured out a way to reverse the process. In doing so, you invented the machine that allowed time travel. Is there anything you would like to ask before I go on?" he asked.

"Yes, do you have any water?"

"Sergeant!" he yelled.

Seconds later, Hightower opened the door.

"Yes, General?"

"Get us some water and a jug of that wine you have stashed under your bunk," Mallory said.

I pulled the letter Hightower had given me out of my pocket. "Is Karen really my wife in the future?"

Mallory chuckled. "Yes," he said.

"Why is she chained to the bed?"

Before he could answer, Hightower came in with a bucket of water and a jug of wine. He handed Mallory the jug and me a dipper and held the water bucket out in front of me. I filled the dipper, drank it down, and handed it back. Hightower left the room without saying anything.

"Are you going to answer my question?" I asked.

"Yes, but first, I want you to know that it's because of you all of this is happening," he said.

My patience was running thin, and I guess he knew so as I stood up and walked toward him; his eyes widened, and I saw the fear. I reached down, grabbed the wine out of his hands, took a long swallow, then handed back the jug. I pulled the chair closer to him before I sat down.

"Okay, tell me about it," I said.

He looked at me, wondering, and started to talk. However, he began with a question that unnerved me even more than I already was.

"In your real-time, what day is it?" he asked.

"June 11, 2015," I said curtly.

Undaunted by my response, he found some inner strength to overcome his fearful look and continued to talk.

"You were on your way to work at a trailer plant where you installed computers so people could check the security of their homes from their phones," he paused as if he wanted me to say something.

"Yes?" I asked.

"It was on this day in 2015 that you made a left turn. Your truck ran head-on into another truck, and you almost died. You ended up in a wheelchair. The doctors said you would never walk again, so you tried to kill yourself. At the time, while still in the hospital, you cut one of the main arteries in your leg. Karen was your doctor. It was she who found you and saved your life. It was she who finally talked some sense into you and made you realize that even though you couldn't walk, life was still worth living.

Her father works at NIFS. He gave you your job. Let's see, this was in the year 2020, five years after the accident. You and Karen were already married, and it was 2022 when you and I built a time machine. You had this idea in your head that you could go back to the day of your accident and prevent it from happening.

I knew it wouldn't work. Karen knew it wouldn't work. So, Karen came up with the idea to send herself back so she could warn you. The problem was that Karen decided to rethink the situation. She wasn't sure that if you never had the accident, the two of you would have met, putting her in a catch .22 situation. One night, she and I were inside the machine. We were working on a component that would allow us to intercept you before the accident. It would bring you to the year 2022, so Karen could tell you everything and ensure that the two of you would meet. Then she would send you back to 2015. It was you who came in and started the machine. You thought we had gone home. I guess you were going to send yourself back, but instead, you sent Karen and me to 1857.

For three months, she and I have traveled over this country, looking for the right components to build a machine that could send us back. We've created a machine, but we are unsure if it will send us back to the right time. Karen said it didn't matter. She wants to leave this place no matter where she may end up. Twice she tried to enter the machine, and I had to stop her. It's why I have her chained to the bed."

Mallory stopped talking and looked at me.

"Okay, let's say I believe you. Now, you can let Karen go," I said.

Mallory stood up, slamming the jug of wine down on his desk. "Look, Jason. This isn't about Karen. She will be okay for now. It's about you and me building a machine to take us to the year 2022," he said.

I stood up, facing him. "No, it's not. It's about sending the two of you to the year 2022. I'll get off in the year 2015," I said.

I saw the smile come to his face. "Now, you're talking. Come with me," he said.

When we walked out of the building, I realized we were no longer at the fort. There were six wooden buildings, all in a row. I saw my truck sitting in front of the last building with its hood up. Hightower stood beside it, holding the alternator. When we passed by him, Mallory held out his hands. Hightower handed him the alternator. We walked up to the door of the building, and Mallory stepped aside, allowing me to open it. Before he stepped in, he looked over at Hightower. How would Hightower know what an alternator was?

"Go get the woman. Lock her inside my office, and don't let her out of your sight," he said.

The first thing I saw was a large roll of copper wire wrapped around a metal rod, and the rod had a handle for turning. Two ends of the wire ran into a ten-foot wooden box. I opened the door to the box. There were several more rods wrapped with wire inside. The floor of the box was covered in what looked like gold. Mallory placed his hand on my shoulder.

"This, my friend, is how I got you here, and this is how we will all go back to where we came from. Turning this wire, I could generate 8 volts. It was enough to get you here but not enough voltage to send us back. I need fourteen more volts, thus…." he held up the alternator.

Taking in everything he said, and after glancing at all that was around me, I replied, "Okay, I get it. The alternator will create the voltage. So, what do we do now?"

"We really need a phone. I searched you while you were out," Mallory stated.

I held up my hand. "It's in the truck's glove box, but you understand, cell towers haven't been invented yet?" I asked. Mallory laughed at this.

"Yes, I know. All I need is the keypad."

"What do you need me to do?"

Mallory walked over and opened the door. "Look, pal, I got this. I know exactly what has to be done and how to do it, so why don't you go over to my office and meet your wife." Not sure if I should trust him, I tilted my head to one side, looking at him. "Hey, man. Trust me. In a few hours, we'll all be home." Not convinced, but knowing this was out of my scope of knowledge, I had to comply.

As soon as I stepped out of the building, the words Karen had said came back to my mind. "He's crazy. I heard him tell his men as soon as they got what he needed, they were to kill you." I remembered the small window at the back of what Mallory called his office. I eased my way around the building and looked inside. Karen lay across the desk. Hightower sat with the end of his chair leaned up against the wall. His rifle was propped up beside the door. I walked back around to the front of the building, opened the door, stepped inside, and picked up the rifle.

"Woah, Woah, Woah. What are you doing?" Hightower asked.

"Just taking a few precautions. Now, if you make any sudden movements, I will shoot you. Do you understand?" I said. Hightower nodded his head.

"Now, I want you to stand up, turn around, and face the wall," I continued.

Hightower didn't hesitate. As soon as he turned around, I whacked him on the back of his head. He fell to the floor. I searched his pockets, found the key, and unlocked the shackles on Karen's legs; she jumped up and wrapped her arms around my neck.

"I knew you would come for me. Where is Mallory?" she asked.

"He's working on the machine. He said we could all go home in a few hours." Karen shook her head.

"It's not the real machine; he's an idiot. The real machine is back at the fort. Did you give him your phone?" she asked. I nodded my head. "Then we need to go. If he tries what he has in mind, he will destroy the machine, and we will all be stuck here."

"How far is the fort?" I asked.

"Not far. We can take your truck." This time I shook my head.

"No, we can't. Mallory had Hightower take it apart."

"Damn, damn, damn!" she said. She grabbed my hand, then she looked me in the eyes. "I know you won't understand why, and I never thought I would say this to you, but let's run." She ran as fast as she could. She was a lot faster than me, but I managed to stay close behind her.

We ran for at least a mile before she stopped. Finally, I saw the fort, the gate was opened, and two men with rifles were standing guard.

"What do we do now?" I asked.

"We are going to walk right up to them. The one on the right is a teenage boy named Edward. He wouldn't kill a fly. The other guy's name is Mark; his wife just had her sixth baby, so he isn't going to put up any kind of fight. You may have to hit him to take his rifle. I will talk them into helping us," Karen said.

Her plan worked like a charm. I didn't even have to hit Mark. He gave me his rifle and led the way to the building. Surprisingly, Mallory was inside, working on the machine. Karen and I walked in. Mallory was stunned by our appearance, aware of my rifle. I wasn't pointing the firearm at Mallory, but his expression showed the same fear from our previous interaction. I knew at once, as I looked around, what his plans were. I saw several hundred gold bars stacked along the wall.

Mallory stopped what he was doing, walked over to a chair, and sat down. He looked up at me.

"What can I say? I lied. You and I are not now, nor were we ever really best friends. And, yes, it was you and her who invented the machine. Your mistake was allowing me to help you put it together and teaching me how it works. Hey, you were the first to use it. You went back to the seventeen hundreds. You brought back a few gold coins. So, you see, you gave me the idea to use the machine as a get-rich-quick scheme. And, no, the two of you didn't want anything to do with my plan. You were too busy trying to figure out a way to warn yourself about the accident, but she was so worried that if you did, the two of you would never meet. It was so, so sad," he said condescendingly. "The two of you were pathetic. I took all I could take. One night, I thought both of you were gone, so I set the machine to this time. I had read in a history book where some outlaws had robbed a large gold shipment. They hid it inside a cave, and it wasn't found until the nineteenth century. I found the gold right where the book said it would be. I used the other machine you saw to melt the gold, molding it into those bars. Anyway, on that night, you had gone home, but she was still there. Now, I didn't force her into this, and it didn't take me long to figure out it was a mistake. It was me who decided to bring you here before you had the accident. I thought maybe the two of you could spend some time together as a normal couple. If you want to know more, then ask her. So, what? I was greedy! You know it doesn't need to end this way! We can all take this gold and go home. I'll take my cut, and the two of you will never have to see me again," he said.

Without saying a word, Karen walked out the door. A few minutes later, she returned with Mark and Hightower. She pointed toward the gold bars. "Take him, lock him up somewhere for now, and all of this gold is yours." Mallory kicked and screamed like a child. He called Karen a traitor as they drug him out of the building.

Karen looked over at me. 'We need to talk."

Not knowing what she had in mind, but if she knew the way back to 2015, I was willing to listen. Karen walked over and sat down in the chair Mallory had previously occupied. She looked up at me with tears in her eyes. "It was true what he said about you going back in time and bringing back those gold coins. What he left out of the story is the part about you not remembering where you'd gone or how you got the coins. So, the chances are, neither of us will remember any of this."

She bowed her head and covered her face with her hands. I placed both hands on her shoulders. "Look... this situation could work out to our advantage," I said.

Karen stood up, wiping her eyes with her hands. She took a step back away from me. "There is something else you should know. Mallory and I... we both knew."

I reached out for her. She took another step back.

"Please, let me finish. We both knew about the gold. Mallory wanted to come by himself, but I insisted I come with him. We lied to you. This is the third time you have come here. It was you who figured out a way to open the magnetic field and intercept yourself before you had the accident. It's how Mallory knew where you would be when he sent those men after you."

This time, I sat down in the chair. I was more confused than before. "Okay, explain to me what happened the other two times I came here."

"I never saw you. You were killed by the Rebels the first time. I believe it was Mallory who killed you the second," she said.

"Why are the two of you still here?" I asked.

She started laughing. She pointed her finger. "Look over there. Do you see the machine? Mallory and I have killed one another ten times each. When we die, we go back to the year 2022. We wrote letters instructing our future selves to bring back parts for the machine. You see, when you die here, whatever you carry in your pockets goes back with you. Even though we brought back the parts, we couldn't get the machine to work. It's why you were allowed to live. We need your help."

"I see, so you need me to set the right coordinates, allowing us and the gold to go back to 2022," I said.

"Not us, just the gold," she said.

"Oh, I see now. We send the gold, then one of us will kill the other and then off ourselves, and we all end up back where we came from. But, this time, we are rich. Only, I'll be in a wheelchair and won't remember any of this."

Karen shook her head. "No, it doesn't have to end this way. I have gone over this a hundred times in my head. You can set the coordinates to the year 2015. You can write yourself a letter warning you about the accident, but if you do, then there's a chance you and I never meet." I walked over to the machine. It all came clear to me. I turned back, facing Karen.

"Now, I see that you keep going over this in your head. It's about the gold. If you and I never meet, then this machine will never exist, and therefore, no gold."

"You're right. But, Jason, listen to me. In the year 2022, I love you. I told you repeatedly that it didn't matter to me that you're in that stupid chair. You can believe this or not. It's your choice, so here is what I want you to do. Write yourself a letter, get inside the machine, and set the coordinates for the year 2015. But, before you do, take the rifle and shoot me in the head. This will leave you with one more choice. You can either kill Mallory or let him fend for himself. Please, whatever you are going to do, do it now," she said.

***

Today started like most others. My old truck did start on the first try. I backed out onto the street then pulled the gear shift down into drive. This time there was no sun in my eyes. I smiled as I reached down in the seat beside me and rubbed a big, shiny bar of gold.

ALL THIS TIME

CHAPTER 8

The bright light hurt my eyes, making me blind for thirty minutes after the blast. The wind blew two hundred miles per hour. If I hadn't been inside the sewer drain, I would have died. When I came out, I couldn't believe what I saw. Nothing was left standing except a few scattered trees across barren land. As far as my eyes could see, it was as if the whole world had blown away.

I walked for who knows how long before I saw the building. It stood alone in the middle of a field. I wondered why it, too, had not been blown away? I walked inside and was struck on the head. To this day, I still don't know with what. I do know that my lights went out, and when I came to, there she stood—the best-looking woman I had ever seen. My feet and hands were tied. I tried, but for the life of me, I couldn't get free.

She didn't say anything for a long time. Then, out of the blue, she asked if I wanted a drink of water. Contemplating the situation and her open invitation to talk, I did my talking. I told her I was on her side. Hell, I really didn't know what side she was on, nor if there were even any sides at all. I told her if she wanted to live, more than likely, she would need my help. I believe this is what convinced her, because it was then that she cut me free. She handed me a bottle of water and a piece of stale bread. I didn't complain. The truth be told, I couldn't think of the last time I had eaten, and when I thought about it, hell, I couldn't even remember my own name.

The weather was unpredictable. It would be freezing one minute, then all at once, it was so hot we could barely stand it. We stayed inside the building for the rest of the night. The following morning, we started walking. I don't think either of us knew where we were going, but we both knew that we might die if we didn't find food and water soon.

It was getting close to dark when we came across the two unappetizing animals. The woman called them to her. The animals and I, too, perceived they had found a friend until the woman pulled out a knife and cut one of their throats. The other one ran away. I stood and watched for over an hour as she picked up the wood, built a fire, and cooked the animal's hind legs. She cut off a significant portion and handed it to me. I had heard of people eating their meat, but not like this. I took a small bite. Either I was hungry, or it wasn't as bad as I thought. Before I knew it, I had finished off the whole piece.

She packed up what was left of the animal, and we continued to walk. It was well into the night when we came to a small lake. She took off her pack, then knelt to taste the water. She cupped her hands, allowing a small amount to cover her palm. She brought her hand to her nose and sniffed the clear liquid. She put it to her mouth, allowing only the tip of her tongue to touch the water. I knew everything was okay when she plunged her face into the lake. It didn't take me long to follow suit. I drank until I thought my stomach was going to burst.

She built a fire and placed the remains of the animal next to it, then, without looking at me, she stripped off all of her clothes and dove into the lake. I had never been much on modesty, so again, I followed suit. I stripped naked and dove in beside her. Each time I tried to swim close to her, she moved away. I tried talking to her, but she wouldn't even acknowledge that I was anywhere on the same planet.

I stayed in the water for a few more minutes, then crawled out and got dressed. I cut off a piece of the animal, then sat down on the ground. Although it was dark, I could make out her body's shape as she came out of the lake. She put on her clothes, ate some of the meat, and then stretched out on the ground next to the fire. I could tell this night wouldn't be any different from the last. It was getting cold. I put more wood on the fire, then I lay down opposite the woman.

I don't know how long I had been asleep when the woman shook me awake. She put her finger to her mouth, letting me know to be quiet. I could hear the faint sound of someone talking. I couldn't tell how many there were, nor what they were saying. The woman grabbed my arm, pulling me toward the lake. We eased our way down the side of the lake until we were able to hide behind a fallen tree. I counted three men, all dressed alike and all carrying rifles.

I felt the woman touch my arm. I could see the fear in her eyes. I told her not to worry. I wasn't going to let them hurt us. She reached inside her pack and brought out a .357 revolver. I checked the cylinder; there were only three bullets. This meant I needed to make every shot count.

We watched as the three men reached our camp. The fire was still burning. One of the men held up his hand and motioned for the others to spread out. They walked in a wide circle around our camp but never came close to us. I guessed they thought they had scared us off. Taking off their packs, they put down their rifles, ate some kind of food, and then lay down. It surprised me that they didn't post a guard. It wasn't long until we heard one of them snoring.

I slid across the ground like a snake. The revolver was cocked and ready to fire. I had never fired a gun, much less killed anyone. I didn't know why I was doing it. I just knew I had to. I was only five feet away when I stood up. I pointed the gun at the closest man and pulled the trigger. The gun sounded like a cannon as the bullet tore through the man's head. In a matter of seconds, I fired the other two shots. All three men were dead. I was standing in the same spot when the woman walked up beside me. From that point on, I started giving the orders. The woman didn't seem to mind, and she did everything I asked.

We took their rifles and extra bullets. The food supply wasn't plentiful, but every little bit helped. We filled their canteens with water, and once again, we were on our way to wherever.

We walked along the banks of the lake. We didn't see or hear anyone else. It seemed like, except for the two of us, the whole world was dead. I kept thinking there had to be others. I wondered where those three men came from. We came to the end of the lake. As we walked on, I looked back. I knew the food and water we carried wouldn't last. I also knew there was still the possibility we could both die.

I couldn't or didn't want to believe what I knew to be the truth. I knew something terrible happened to our world. All I could remember was the blast. I didn't know how I had gotten into that sewer drain. I couldn't remember where I was from. I couldn't even remember my own name. I finally got the woman to carry on a normal conversation, only to find out that she didn't remember much more than me. She remembered being inside a metal container. There were two men in there with her. They held her down and took turns with her. She managed to get one of their guns and killed them both. She also let me know that if I tried to touch her in the wrong way, she would kill me too.

For six days, we walked. Eventually, we found a small town. We waited until dark and then snuck in behind one of the buildings. The smell was horrible. I figured it to be the odor of the dead. The woman handed me a piece of cloth. I didn't know why until I saw her tie one around her mouth and nose.

We walked to the front of the building, and the door stood open. I went in first. There were eight people inside. It seemed they had taken something which had caused their death. They were sitting in a circle holding hands. I could tell they had been dead a while, for the heat had caused their bodies to swell and rot.

We found plenty of food and water inside the other buildings, but the only people were the dead ones in the first building. The small town didn't seem to be affected by the blast. I wondered where all the people had gone and why.

I gave the woman a name. I called her Belle. Silently, I thought I must have come from the south because my first thought was Southern Belle, then I decided to settle on Belle for short. I never knew and never asked how she picked the name for me. She started calling me Jack, and I always answered her.

We picked out one of the houses near the end of the town and stocked it with all the canned food we could find. The house had a well behind it, so we also had plenty of water. I found three generators inside the hardware store and went to one of the two gas stations for gasoline. I figured out how to fill the generators with gas, but Belle figured out how to wire the generator to the house.

There was already a TV and a VCR in the house, and Belle came up with at least three hundred movies. I let her pick out what she wanted to watch. It seemed I would have picked the same ones anyway.

I guess we had been in the town for about three months when we saw a plane fly over. I wanted to travel in the direction the plane had come from, but Belle wouldn't leave. She said it would be too dangerous, and we should stay where we were until someone came for us.

We started keeping up with the days. We had been in the small town for seven months when Belle asked if I would marry her. She had watched a videotape with two people getting married and stated that if we said the same words, we too would be married. When I asked Belle why, she couldn't explain and simply said, "I want to be married before I die."

It was then that I realized why Belle thought the two of us would never leave the town. I discovered the book Belle had been reading about nuclear explosions. The book said exposed people usually died within one year of some kind of cancer.

The next day we got married in front of the TV set. Belle had cleaned a vacant room at a motel in town. I set up the generator so we would have lights. We stayed for two days, then went back to our house.

One day, Belle came running into the house. She grabbed my arm, pulling me toward the door. When we got outside, I saw a truck coming towards us. I pushed Belle back inside the house and shut the door. I wanted to be sure, whoever they were, they wouldn't harm us. We watched three men and two women climb out of the truck. They walked from building to building as if they thought they would find someone. They were a block away from our house. I guess Belle couldn't contain herself.

She ran past me and out the door. All three men and both women came running toward her. One of the men pulled a gun from under his coat and fired two shots. The first shot knocked Belle back through the door. I grabbed one of our rifles as one of the men appeared at the door. I shot him in his chest, and he fell back on the porch. It was then I went crazy. I didn't think of them shooting me. I ran out the door, not really aiming the rifle at anyone. I fired until it wouldn't fire anymore, and when I came to my senses, they were all dead.

I stood staring at the dead bodies until Belle's image falling through the door came into my head. I ran inside the house, picked her up, and lay her on the table. To my relief, she was alive. The bullet had lodged in her chest. She was bleeding badly. I knew I had to do something. I ran to the doctor's building. Not knowing what I was looking for, I grabbed a small black bag. I ran back to the house and emptied the bag on the floor. I picked up a sharp knife and a pair of tweezers. I cut a hole in Belle's breast. Using the tweezers, I poked around in the hole until I hit something hard. I grabbed the bullet and pulled it out of her. Just as I finished sewing up the wound, she opened her eyes. She opened her mouth, trying to talk, but no words came out. A few seconds later, she went back to sleep. I stayed by her side for the next three days. She was in and out most of the time. For a while, I thought she was going to be alright, but on the fourth day, Belle died.

I buried her in the backyard behind our house. There was no reason for me to stay any longer, so I loaded the truck with food, water, and two five-gallon cans of gas. I waited until dark then drove out of town.

Two hours later, I ended up here. All this time, we were two hours away from civilization. All this time, I could have driven Belle to a real hospital. I loved her, and I miss her a lot. I guess it's why I tried to kill myself. I think it's why they have put me in this place. Was the bright light and blast a knock at death's door? I arose from bed as I had been allowed the privilege to walk the hall and ultimately outside. Walking through the double doors to the outside of my residence, I watched the birds fly over. To my left, I saw beautiful buildings aligned across the road. I noticed the black-decorated welded fence that either kept me in or kept others out. Dismissing the thought, I took a walk toward the grounds garden. The wind blew, and a sweet fragrance greeted me. I continue walking only to find myself at the front of my residence since my suicide attempt. The sign outside read *Harris County Mental Hospital*.

A CONSCIOUS JOURNEY

CHAPTER 9

I was standing in front of a sporting goods store, looking through the window at some new rods and reels when she walked by. I saw only her reflection, but I could tell she was upset. I told myself not to get involved, but I've always been a sucker when it came to beautiful women. I called out, asking if she needed any help. When she turned around, I saw her eyes wide with fear. I told the woman she need not be afraid; I only wanted to help. It wasn't until she turned and ran that I knew it wasn't me, but the three men who were running toward us that frightened her. My first mistake... well, no, my first mistake was allowing myself to notice the woman. My second mistake was stepping into the path of the oncoming men.

As I was picking myself up from the sidewalk, I saw the woman turn the corner at the side of the building. I kept telling myself to let her go. I was already bleeding from a silver dollar-sized hole where the sidewalk had erased the skin from my arm. I climbed into my truck. Instead of going in the same direction as the woman and her pursuers, I chose to take the opposite direction around the building. At the back, I saw the woman running toward my truck. The three men were close behind her. I spun my truck around, put the gear lever in reverse, and backed toward her.

I was within 15 feet or so of her when I slammed on the brakes. I reached over to open the door but felt the woman's weight as she dove into the back of my truck. Without taking the time to look back, I pulled the gear lever down into drive and stepped on the gas. It was five miles outside of town before I stopped the truck. By the time I got out, the woman was standing by my door. I asked if she was OK. She shook her head from side to side, then told me we needed to get moving. She said if those men caught up to her, they would probably kill her, then her reason for being here in this life would be lost. I had no idea what she was talking about. I took her arm, led her around to the truck's passenger side, opened the door, and pointed toward the seat.

I drove another 10 miles then pulled into a service station. Neither of us spoke a single word, and I was kind of creeped out by the way this woman looked at me. I bought some gas and two Sprites. When I got back in the truck, I twisted the cap off one of the drinks and handed it to the woman. Again, she said we needed to get moving. She said those men chasing her were smart and were somehow tracking her every move. I asked her why the men were chasing her. She said once we were someplace safe, she would explain everything to me.

A half-hour later, I pull into the driveway of my home. The house consists of four bedrooms, a library, living room, dining room, kitchen, washroom, and a three-car garage. It's built next to one of the largest lakes in Alabama. The woman walked from room to room until she had inspected every one of them. Then she walked down to the lake and went inside the boathouse where I kept my pontoon and bass boats.

I watched as she walked back toward the house. I had made a pot of beef stew the night before. I ladled out two bowls, set them on the table, and then poured two glasses of iced tea. I sat down and started eating. The woman followed suit. I waited for us to finish our meal before asking her the several questions I had in mind. But before we finished, I heard the doorbell. The woman raised her head and looked at me. I stood up, and again she followed suit. I held up my hand and told her to stay put. I walked to the front door and looked through the peephole. I saw the three men who were chasing the woman standing outside. I ran back to the kitchen. The sliding glass door, which led out onto my back deck, stood open. I caught a glimpse of the woman as she entered the boathouse. Less than a minute later, I watched in awe as my new bass boat raced away from the shore.

The three men came around the side of my house. One of them pulled out a gun and fired three shots toward the fleeing boat. I didn't know what to expect, but I wasn't taking any chances. I ran back inside, closed the sliding glass door, then went to the hall closet and loaded my shotgun. Holding the gun out in front of me, I eased my way back down the hall. When I stepped out into the open, all three men were standing outside the glass door. One of them held up a badge. From that distance, I couldn't tell what branch of law enforcement he was from, so I propped the gun up against the wall, walked over, and opened the door.

Two of the men came inside. They wanted to know how I knew the woman. When I told them, I didn't really know her, they wanted to know why I was willing to risk my own life for someone I didn't know. Instead of answering their questions, I asked some of my own. I wanted to know what in the world this woman could have done to cause them to want to kill her on sight. The men denied trying to kill her, but had a hard time answering my next question. I asked him why he had fired his gun at my boat. He thought for a few moments, then realized I had given him an out. He said I was exactly right. He wasn't shooting at the woman; he was shooting at my boat. They wanted to know what type of boat it was, how much gas was in the tank, and where the next loading dock was located. After I satisfied their questions, they gave me a card with a phone number on it, and without telling me why they were after this woman, they left. I watched until their car was out of sight, then ran out to my boathouse. I started the pontoon's engine, then headed downriver. I tried calculating the time from when the woman had left my house until now, but I knew that my guess of thirty minutes could be wrong.

I scanned both sides of the lake in case she had decided to abandon the boat and knew my hunch was right on target when I saw my boat at the back of a small slew. The water wasn't deep enough for me to go inside the slew with my pontoon, and the growth at the edges was too thin to walk on. Even though I didn't see the woman, I yelled for her to bring the bass boat out of the slew.

To my surprise, she sat up inside the boat and used one of the paddles to turn the boat around. She started the engine and drove back toward me. When she was close enough, I told her the men had left, and it was safe for her to return my boat.

I turned the pontoon around and told her to follow me, but the bass boat was much faster than the pontoon's thirty miles per hour top speed, so it wasn't long before she passed me. When I got back to my house, my bass boat was tied inside the boathouse, but the woman was nowhere in sight. I searched the house, the yard, the woods on both sides of the house, and I even drove several miles in both directions. It was like she had just disappeared. I decided to put the woman out of my mind and carry on with my life.

It was the very next day, at about the same time as the day before, I stood in front of the same sporting goods store, looking at the same reel and rods when I saw the woman's reflection as she walked by the same window. The first thing that went through my mind was the movie *Groundhog Day*, in which Bill Murray woke up every morning only to repeat the day before. I yelled for the woman to stop. She turned around and asked if I was talking to her. I looked over my shoulder, half expecting the three men to be there, but I didn't see them. When I looked back at the woman, I realized I had made a mistake. This woman had the same long brown hair and even had big brown eyes, but it wasn't the woman from the day before. I told the woman I was sorry. I thought she was someone else, then I quickly turned and walked into the store.

I walked around inside the store. I couldn't get the woman out of my mind. I even tried telling myself the events from the day before never happened. This worked for a while because it was then that I remembered why I had come to the sporting goods store that day in the first place. I walked over and picked out not one but two of the new rods and reels.

Two days later, I was still trying to wrap my head around what had happened. I knew it was real because I had the man's card, and my bass boat had two bullet holes in its side. As a matter of fact, I was patching the holes when the woman walked into my boathouse. I tilted my head and looked into her big, brown eyes. Without saying a word, she turned and walked out. Seconds later, I was right on her heels. Once we were inside the house, she said she was hungry and asked if I minded fixing her a sandwich while she took a shower. I started to stop her and demand she answer some questions, but then realized she wore the same clothes as she'd had on that first day, and her hair was a tangled mess. Instead, I just turned and walked into the kitchen.

Exactly one hour and twelve minutes later, she walked into the kitchen wearing a pair of my sweat pants and one of my tee shirts. We sat in silence while she ate until I couldn't take it anymore. I slammed my hand down on the table. I told her I had been very calm about this whole situation, but I wanted her to answer all of my questions. I wanted to know who, where, and why. Who was she? Where had she come from? And why were those men chasing her? She answered my questions all right. And let me tell you, her answers blew my mind. She answered the why question first. She said we didn't need to worry about those men because she tracked them down and took care of them when she left. I couldn't bring myself to ask her what she meant by that. She said she was here in search of me and that she'd been here for several months. She had lived off the land for a while as a homeless person but decided she could do better by robbing a bank. Those men were chasing her because she had no choice when she killed the bank guard. Once again, my mind started racing, then she stunned me with the who and the where. She said she was my wife in another life, and she figured out a way to cross the realms of consciousness. She believed she had figured out a way to take the two of us back to where she had begun her conscious journey. Even though I didn't ask her how she answered the unasked question regardless. She said everyone shares the same conscious mind, and we always have and we always will. She said not only do we live many lives before this one, but we also live many lives after this one. I, myself, had studied yoga meditation and had read about future and past lives, but nowhere have I read where it was possible for us to live several lives simultaneously. She said at times, we are able to remember parts of our past lives, as well as the other lives we are now living. Then she asked if I had ever seen her in my dreams. I told her it might be possible, but I don't remember many of my dreams. I saw then that she was starting to get angry. She said either I believed her or I didn't. She had put herself through pure hell trying to find me because she loved me and wanted to convince me to journey across our consciousness, and the both of us would return to our lives where she had begun this journey.

I looked around and thought about my life at that point in time. I was a single male living alone in a beautiful home with six figures in the bank, a car, a truck, and two boats. Then I took another good look at the woman. She was what I considered a really good-looking woman, the long brown hair and big brown eyes. She was around twenty-one or twenty-two with an hourglass figure. I thought about it some more. Even with all this going for her, I still couldn't bring myself to comply with her request. I gave her my reason and told her my decisions, and once again, she blew my mind. She wanted to know if she remained in this, her third level of consciousness, would I be willing to spend the rest of this life together.

Instead of answering her question, I asked her another one of my own.

"If the two of us could travel back to where you started and if I decided I don't like it, Will it be possible for me to return home to this life?"

As I waited for her answer, another thought crossed my mind, and I didn't know why it had taken me so long to figure this out. *If she wanted me to go back as her husband, then something happened?*

Being rather frank, I quickly asked another question. "What happened to me?"

She looked at me with a peculiar face. Nodding her head as if in agreement, she sighed before talking, "Fair enough, you have a right to know. Yes, something did happen."

She continued to give an account stating that she and I wanted to leave that particular life for a better one. In the process, we were separated because my death had come before hers. She said she couldn't promise if we traveled through our levels of consciousness together if we would ever be able to return to this life.

I shook my head from side to side, not liking her answer. Finally, I told her my point on reasoning and my decision to remain in my own life. She had already confessed to committing murder. Considering that, I didn't believe it would be possible for the two of us to spend our lives together.

I saw the tears come into her eyes. She told me she was going to use the bathroom. She stood up and walked out of the room. The next time I saw her, she held my shotgun out in front of her. I felt the blast hit me in the center of my chest. The last thing I remember of that life was my chair flipping over backward.

***

I saw the train coming down the tracks. I could have set any watch by its time. Every night, I drove parallel to the tracks while on my way to the rubber factory where I worked as a laborer. This night, my wife's last words were on my mind. She wanted a better life and thought she had figured out a way for us to have it.

I didn't know if I had slowed down or the train had sped up. I had always been able to cross the tracks exactly thirty seconds before the train arrived at the crossing, but on this night, the train's engine caught the rear end of my truck, causing the cab to spin sideways and slam into the side of the train. I don't believe I ever lost consciousness, although I did have a strange image of my wife holding a shotgun pointed toward my chest.

I remember the thump, thump, thump sound as the train cars passed me by. I remember the silence after the last train car went by. I don't know how long I was trapped inside my truck when a man was telling me to hold on and that he had called for help.

I remember the ambulance ride, then being rolled into the hospital on the gurney. I remember bright lights. Two men and three women were cutting off my clothes. I was there and could see and hear everything.

They were talking about me. In my mind, they should have been speaking to me. It seemed my left leg was broken below my knee, and I was still bleeding from a big hole in the back of my head. I heard this ringing sound in my ears, then one of the men pressed two cold paddles against my chest. The shock that went through my own body was more painful than anything I had ever felt. Then, there she was. My wife telling me to let go so we could have a better life. My ears stopped ringing, and I heard a beep, beep, beep sound coming from somewhere in the room. I heard one of the women talking. I think she said something like, welcome back, or you made it back. Then I remember feeling pain in my leg. I tried to sit up, but two men grabbed my arms and told me to lie still. I saw my wife standing beside me. Her mouth was moving, but I couldn't understand her words. Everyone started yelling. I saw the paddles coming back toward my chest. I felt the pain. The lights faded away. The last thing I remember from that life was my wife holding those cold paddles and smiling down at me.

***

I sat straight up in bed. I must have screamed because my wife came running into the bedroom. I told her about my dreams, of her holding the shotgun, then her holding the type of paddles that doctors use on heart attack patients.

She threw herself on top of me. She kissed my face several times. I was really confused by her following statement because she and I had been together since high school. She said she had found a way to where we would never have to be apart ever again. We made love for hours, then I watched her long brown hair sway back and forth across her naked body as she left the room.

COUNTING MINUTES

CHAPTER 10

I don't know if I was asleep and dreaming or just thinking about my wife and son when I heard the gate open. I looked at the mark on the wall. At first, I counted months, then I counted weeks, then it was days. Only that which gave us all life could help me now; I knew it wouldn't be long before I had to count the minutes. The next sound I heard was two pairs of shoes walking down the long hallway. I knew they weren't coming for me. If they were, there would be more shoes. My heart did race a little when the sound stopped in front of my door. When I saw the white collar of the priest, I let the air out of my lungs. Without speaking, he stepped into my cell. The guard closed and locked the door behind him. He made the cross sign, then asked if I minded if he sat with me for a while. I slid over and patted the side of my bunk. I thought he was going to ask me to confess my sins, but instead, he simply asked how I had gotten myself into this particular situation. He sat down beside me. I don't know how long I talked, but every word I said was the truth. I started with the day I found the dead bodies of my wife and son.

It was the fifth of November, the weather was reasonably sixty-five degrees, but was unseasonably warm. I got up early. I wanted to get my boat in the water before the sun came up. Over the years, it had been my experience that this was the best time to catch the bigger fish. I kissed my wife on her sleeping forehead, then checked on my son. We had planned on him going with me, but he had come down with a cold. He was disappointed until I promised he could go on the next trip.

The day started out great. I was first in line at the boat dock, which allowed me to arrive at my favorite fishing spot before anyone else. Throughout the day, I caught several fish and a couple of softshell turtles. It was almost dark by the time I pulled my boat out of the water.

I stopped at the bait shop. The two young boys who always cleaned my fish met me at my truck. I still remember their smiles when I held up the stringer of fish and their laughter when I showed them the turtles. This always made it worth the one dollar per fish I paid for their services. Sometimes I gave them extra because they had told me the money would go towards their college funds.

I remember how happy I felt up until I parked my truck in the driveway of our home. My wife's car was missing, and it seemed like every light in the house had been left on. I had never known my wife to leave our house without turning off the lights. In my gut, I felt something was wrong. I yelled her name as I walked into the house. When she didn't answer, I felt my stomach churn. I stood still, listening to the normal sounds of the house. We had a clock that hung above the fireplace. I could hear it ticking but couldn't remember ever hearing it before then. I could hear the air blowing from the vents that heated our home. The uncomfortable silence of what I didn't hear allowed me to listen to my heart beating against my chest. All of a sudden, there was a surge of adrenaline that came over me. I took the stairs two at a time, then ran into our bedroom. I don't remember how long I stood there staring at them. I don't even remember calling 911, but the police told me I did.

The sun was already up when I watched people I didn't know put the bodies of my wife and son through the back door of the van. Then, one by one, I watched the police cars drive away. I was told to pack a few things and leave the house until they were finished with their investigation, and when I opened the top drawer of our dresser, I threw up. My wife's words came back to me. She had asked me to not keep a gun in our house. With the gun missing, I knew my wife and son might have been killed with that very same gun.

My mind raced with over a thousand thoughts a second. I believed I knew who had done this, and I knew I should have told the police the truth when they asked if I had any enemies. I didn't pack any clothes. I just took a few water bottles from the fridge and then got into my truck and drove. When the low fuel light started blinking, I realized I had exited Maine and driven into New Hampshire. After refueling the truck and pulling back onto the interstate, I let my mind wander back to where I believed all this had started.

I was in my early forties working on an oil rig in north Texas. I had just finished working a sixteen-hour shift. I stopped at a bar called Driller's Paradise. There were reasons it was called that.

First of all, almost every driller went there to wind down after their shift. Secondly, it was the only bar within a twenty-five-mile radius. Third, it was a place where a person could buy almost anything: alcohol, uppers, downers, even a woman to sleep with you if you were into that. I drank four beers, then got back behind the wheel of my truck, heading back to the one-bedroom trailer I rented for a hundred bucks a week. I still couldn't remember much of the accident's beginning, but I could remember the end results. My truck was embedded in the side of an old Ford Falcon. A young pregnant woman was lying in a puddle of blood inside the mangled wreck.

I was charged with her death, convicted of manslaughter, and sentenced to three years working on one of the Texas Department of Corrections pea farms. During those three years, I received several letters from the young woman's husband telling me of the different ways he was planning to kill my family and me. I wrote to him only once, telling him how sorry I was, and I didn't set out that particular day with the intention of killing his wife and unborn child.

I had planned on finding the man so we could talk. My mother advised me against it. When I got out of prison, I moved back to Maine.

Other than my mother, I had no family. I was an only child, and my father drank himself to death when I was ten years old.

I took a job doing construction, and within one year, three things happened: I met the love of my life and got married, my mother died, leaving me the house, and my son was born. Six years went by after this, and I had never been as happy in my entire life. I had not forgotten about the accident, but I had put it in the back of my mind. Now, I have only one thing on my mind-killing the man I believed killed my wife and son.

I was somewhere in New York when the engine in my truck locked up. I didn't realize the red light had been flashing, letting me know my truck was low on oil. Leaving everything behind, I stepped out of my truck and stuck out my thumb. I got a ride from a man on his way to Atlanta, Georgia. He told me he was going to visit his grandchildren. He did most of the talking, and that was alright with me. I couldn't remember the last time I had slept, and I still don't remember going to sleep, but when the old man woke me, we were in downtown Atlanta.

Although I had driven through Atlanta, I had never stopped. The streets were full of cars. The sidewalk was crowded with people. Everyone seemed to be in a hurry to get to wherever they were going. I was hungry and in dire need of a strong cup of coffee. I had walked several blocks before I found a place where I could eat. Besides the girl behind the counter and myself, there were only three other people inside the shop. There were two young girls. I guessed them to be teenagers, and I wondered why they weren't in school. They sat across from one another at one of the six booths in the shop. The third was a man who looked like he hadn't had a bath in a few days. He sat at a booth close to the exit. I felt like he was watching me, but I figured I was being paranoid. So, I put the thought out of my mind.

I ordered a large black coffee and a Danish. I chose the booth closest to the young girls. I had just finished my coffee and Danish when the girl came from behind the counter, carrying a small pot of coffee. Without asking, she refilled my cup. I thanked her and told her I would be right back. I pulled off my jacket and laid it across the back of the booth. The man looked up at me as I walked past him on my way to the restroom. When I came out, the man was gone, and when I got back to my booth, my jacket was no longer there. I asked the two girls if they had seen the man take my jacket. Both of them looked at me as if I were speaking Chinese. The girl behind the counter said she had her back turned when he went out the door. She said she had a couple of jackets behind the counter where her boss had left them, and she was sure he wouldn't mind if I took one. I took her up on her offer for a jacket as I thought about the weather. I cringed as I explained why I couldn't pay for the coffee.

My wallet containing my money, my credit cards, and my identification was inside the jacket's pocket. She said she was sorry about what had happened and for me not to worry about the coffee.

When I left the coffee shop, I walked several miles before seeing the entrance ramp to the interstate. I had two choices. I could go north, back to Maine, and get more money and proper ID, or I could go south, to Alabama, and then west to where I hoped the man, I was looking for still lived. I chose south.

I walked with my thumb out until the sun was going down. No one seemed to want to pick up a hitchhiker. I crawled under a bridge. There were already a few homeless people camped, so I found a spot no one seemed to want and lay down. I tried clearing my mind by listening to the cars go by above me, but couldn't get the image of my wife and son lying on that blood-soaked bed out of my head. I remember feeling the tears running down my face. The next thing I remembered was someone kicking me on the bottom of one of my feet. When I finally got my eyes opened, two policemen were standing over me. They were polite when they told me I had to move on. I explained to them how I had lost my wallet. They told me I could go down to any police station and file a complaint and give a description of the man, but it was their opinion no one would even look for him. They said I should continue on wherever I was heading. To my surprise, one of the policemen pulled out his own wallet and handed me a five-dollar bill. He told me there was a place two blocks down where I could get an all you could eat breakfast and coffee for five bucks.

I thanked them, then watched as they got into their car and drove away. I decided to hang on to the money. Twenty minutes later, I stood on the side of Interstate 65 with my thumb out. After an hour, with no one even looking my way, I started walking. I had heard an old saying from a man who was giving me directions to a lake. He told me if I went by highway, the lake was five miles away, but if I went as the crow flies, it was only one mile. I looked up. The sun was to my right, so I knew which way I needed to travel. I put the rising sun to my back, crossed the interstate, and walked into the woods.

I crossed several streets, entering more wooded areas. It wasn't long until the streets became dirt roads and, instead of being behind me, the sun was in front of me. I had to zig-zag around houses and farms until I came to a small town. There was only one store, a post office, a garage, and a laundromat. I went inside the store. The old woman behind the counter looked me up and down, then asked if I was lost. I told her I was just passing through. I got a soda, a pack of lunch meat, some mayo, and a small loaf of bread. This left me with eighty-three cents in change.

I walked another day, keeping the sun either directly behind me or directly in front of me. I hurt my leg running from some dogs and spent the night in a tree. Then, I walked another day and well into the night. I walked until I thought I couldn't walk anymore. I didn't believe there was a muscle in my entire body that didn't hurt for one reason or another. When I came to a lake, I sat down on a large rock. I looked at my watch, which read 3:30 a.m. I knew this couldn't be right, because the sun was coming up from behind the trees, so this meant it was some time between six and six-thirty. Then, I heard the sound of some kind of animal to my right. A big splash caused my head to snap back forward. The ripples in the water told me a large fish had snatched something from the surface of the lake. The thought of the fish made me realize I hadn't eaten since the lunch meat and bread ran out. I wondered if it would be possible for me to wade out into the lake and catch a fish with my bare hands. I pushed the thought out of my mind, knowing it wouldn't be.

As soon as I stood up, I felt the pain in my leg. I didn't need to wonder what had happened. I thought back to when the pack of wild dogs tried to make a meal out of me. I pulled a calf muscle while running away. Even now, I don't know how I was able to climb that tree.

I made sure my canteen was full of water, then walked with my back to the sun. The pain in my leg was pretty bad at first, but the further I walked, the better it felt. Out of habit, I kept looking at my watch, knowing good and well it had stopped. The sun wasn't above me, nor in front of me, so I knew it wasn't yet noon. I thought I smelled smoke but wasn't sure. It seemed to be coming from the north. I knew I needed to keep moving west but couldn't resist the temptation of walking in the assumed direction of the smell.

The sky above me darkened. I knew it might rain, as it had for the past days. It never lasted more than a half-hour, then the sun returned. Most people would have said it was hot, but me being from the far north, I always welcomed the heat. It's just a guess to say it was two miles later when I saw the smoke, and also a guess to say it was another mile later when I walked up to the charred remains of an old house. The woman didn't hear me approaching until I was almost upon her, and I didn't see the shotgun until she turned around. She didn't say anything, and neither did I. We just stood there staring at one another. I guessed her to be in her mid-fifties. Her salt and pepper hair had been chopped off short. It looked like she or someone else had cut it with a knife. She wore a long-sleeved pullover shirt and a pair of jeans that were at least two sizes too big for her. There were no shoes on her feet.

The shotgun looked old—a single barrel. I asked if she was going to shoot me. She told me she didn't want to but would if she needed to. I assured her I meant her no harm and wouldn't do anything that would give her a reason.

She lay the shotgun down on the ground, then picked up a shovel. She pointed to a stand of trees, about thirty yards from the house. She told me to dig a hole large enough to bury her dead husband. It was then I noticed him, a charred body next to what used to be the front porch of the house. I didn't say anything. I just walked over to the trees and dug the hole. I don't know how much time had passed. I guessed it to be a couple of hours. We had finished burying her husband and just stood there looking at the grave. It was she who broke the silence. She said he was a good man. I really didn't know what to say, so I told her I was sure he was. She pointed toward the shotgun. She said it was time to do what she was about to do when I walked up. I've never been slow-minded; I knew what she meant. I walked to where she had laid the shotgun, picked it up, and unloaded it. I put the shell in the pocket of my jacket. I told her I wasn't going to let her kill herself, and I would help her find another place to live. She asked me why I would be willing to take time out of my own life to help her. I told her that even though bad things happened, life was still worth living. At that point in time, I didn't know if I believed my own words.

She pointed toward a wooden structure that, at one time, could have been a barn. To me, it looked like it was leaning to the left and might fall down at any minute. She told me there was an old pickup truck inside it. I walked over and swung the doors open as far back as they would go. I wanted to get as much light inside the barn as I could. I realized when the woman had said old pickup truck, she really meant old. It was a 1949 Ford. I raised the hood and saw it had a small six-cylinder engine. I checked the radiator for water and removed the cover from the carburetor. I flipped the spring lever on its side, checking for any sign of fuel. I didn't see any, so I started looking around inside the barn. As it turned out, I found what I was looking for behind the seat of the old truck- a three-foot piece of an old garden hose. I removed the gas cap, stuck one end of the hose down into the tank, and placed my thumb over the other end. I trapped some of the gas inside the hose. I poured a small amount of gas inside the carburetor, then got into the truck, turned the key, and pushed the starter button with my foot. The engine turned over a few times, then it started right up. I replaced the cover, closed the hood, and backed out of the barn. I stopped alongside the woman, reached across the seat, and opened the door for her. She took a couple of steps toward the truck, then stopped and turned around. She looked to where her house had once stood, then looked up toward the trees where we had buried her husband. With tears running down her face, she turned around and got into the truck.

I drove that old truck several miles down a narrow dirt road before coming to a paved highway. The woman told me to turn left, so I did. It was not even a mile later that she pointed to a house. It was a Spanish-style structure made out of white brick. It was about fifty yards off the highway. I pulled into the driveway and stopped. The woman told me she knew the people who lived there. I let the truck roll slowly down the gravel drive until we came to the house.

I sat in the truck and watched as the woman walked up to the front door. Without knocking, she opened the door and walked into the house. A few minutes later, I heard a gunshot. I reached over, grabbed the shotgun, and got out of the truck. I hadn't asked her name, so I just yelled, asking if she was alright. When no one answered, I held the shotgun out in front of me, walked over, and pushed the door open with my foot. I was all the way inside the house when I realized the shell for the shotgun was still in my pocket.

As it turned out, on that day, I didn't need a gun. The shot I heard came from a .38 pistol the woman had used to shoot herself in the head. I found her lying on the floor beside the living room couch. I believe if I had eaten anything, I would have thrown up.

I checked the rest of the house. I didn't find anyone else, dead or alive. The photos hanging on the walls told me that the house belonged to a young couple who could or could not have been related to the woman.

The kitchen was stocked with food, so I helped myself to a canned ham and a stale loaf of bread. There were several bottles of wine sitting on the counter, and before I knew it, I was drunk off my ass and found myself crying. All I could think about was my wife and son. I couldn't stop the tears. I stumbled into one of the bedrooms and lay across the bed.

I didn't know how long I had slept. When I opened my eyes, I thought I was still dreaming because I was staring into the face of a large duck. I don't know if it was from fear or confusion, but I couldn't move a muscle until the duck let out a long, loud sound. Then I found myself falling off the other side of the bed. As it turned out, what I thought was a duck wasn't a duck at all. Instead, it was a very large goose. As soon as I stood, it did a quick turn around and made a honk, honk, honk sound as it ran out of the bedroom. I shook my head to clear the cobwebs, then found the bathroom. I reached into the shower and turned the knob. The water came pouring out. I waited a few minutes, then realized it wasn't going to get hot. When I took off all my clothes and stepped into the shower, the cold water took my breath away. After my body had gotten used to the chill, I looked around. I found soap, shampoo, and some other liquid that smelled like fruit.

After my shower, I walked naked back to the room where I slept. I went through the drawers and closets. I found a lot of clothes, but they were all too small for me. It was in the next bedroom I found what I needed. I chose a pair of blue jeans and a black pullover shirt. The brown hiking boots were one size too big, so I put on an extra pair of socks. I looked at myself in a full-length mirror. I counted back the days. It had been twelve days since I had left my home in Maine. I didn't recognize the man who stared back at me. Once again, tears ran down my face. I couldn't shake the feeling of my wife's and son's death being my fault. If only I hadn't gone fishing. I would have been home when he came into our house.

It was the honking sound of the goose that brought my thoughts back to reality. When I took a step toward the goose, it turned and walked away. I followed it into the kitchen. The goose stood over what looked like a dog's double feeding bowl. I filled one side with water from the tap and the other with crackers from a box that I found inside one of the cabinets. I reached down and patted the goose on its head before leaving the room.

Once again, I went through the house. This time I looked for money, and I found several hundred dollars in a shoebox under one of the beds. There was also a .38 pistol exactly like the one the poor woman had used to kill herself. I found a small tote bag in the closet and filled it with two more sets of clothes. I lay the pistol on top of the clothes before zipping the bag shut. I went back into the kitchen. I didn't know where, but the goose had gone. I filled an empty milk jug with water and carried the tote bag and water out to the truck. I thought about carrying the woman back and burying her beside her husband. Although I felt terrible, I decided to move on. I was looking for one man, and I believed I knew where he lived. At that point in time, I was still at least three thousand miles away from him.

The old truck rattled and shook as I drove down the highway. I stayed on the back road, avoiding cities until I got to Mobile, Alabama. I noticed every truck and car that passed. People were staring at me. Every time I had to stop at a light or make a turn, people turned and pointed. It wasn't until the man standing on the sidewalk yelled and asked what model she was, did I realize I was attracting too much attention. I left the truck sitting at a rest stop once I made it through the tunnel that ran under the Mobile Bay and into the state of Mississippi.

I walked alongside the interstate for several miles and thought about going into the woods to camp for the night when a semi-truck pulled to a stop in front of me. I climbed up, opened the door, and slid into the passenger seat. I placed the tote bag on the floor between my feet, then unzipped the tote a little, so I would be able to get to the pistol if I needed it.

The driver was a young woman. She was as big around as she was tall. She asked where I was heading. When I told her I was on my way to California, she laughed. She told me I was a lucky man because she was on her way to Nevada and would welcome the company. I asked her how long it would take to reach her destination. She said if I knew how to drive her rig, we could be there in three days. I told her I had worked in the oil fields where I had moved semis around the yard but had never driven one on the open road.

She smiled and said I wouldn't have any problems with her rig because it had an automatic tranny. I dozed off to sleep. When I woke, we were somewhere in Texas. She pulled the rig up next to the pumps at a truck stop. I told her I had money and could help pay for the fuel. She pulled a credit card from the side pocket on the door and assured me the company she drove for paid for everything she needed.

I did pump the fuel, then met her inside. We both ordered ham and eggs. I drank black coffee while she drank beer. She ordered two beers to go. I looked across the table at her.

She laughed and told me not to worry because I would be driving her rig for the next several hours. I managed to make it from the parking lot of the truck stop up onto the interstate. She said she was satisfied that

I would be able to handle things, then bid me goodnight and crawled into the truck's sleeper bed. A few minutes later, she stuck her head out from behind the curtain.

"If you feel the need to pull this rig over to the side of the interstate, you can crawl back here with me."

Not sure how to take her, I swallowed a lump in my throat and rushed out my words.

"I don't believe that will be necessary. I am married."

She looked at me and turned her head sideways as if she were collecting her thoughts, and then she burst out laughing.

"I don't mean in that way, silly. Plus, you are not my type gender-wise," she stated as she looked at the mid-thigh section of my pants. Nodding her head in acknowledgment of my gender, she raised her eyes, locking them with mine, and with a bit of attitude, she continued

"If you get my meaning." She smiled a little. I am thinking about our safety. Sooo, please pull my rig over if you get sleepy. That is all I am asking."

I nodded my head in agreement, and she retreated behind the curtain. I didn't know I was holding my breath. I exhaled and started the rig. I remembered a previous conversation about her sexual needs.

She stressed that it was a help to have me travel with her, and she had no intentions of having sex with me to pay for my ride.

I drove seven straight hours before stopping at another truck stop. I used the woman's credit card to refuel the truck. I paid for my own food with some of the money I took from the shoe box. While I was eating, she came in carrying a gym bag and told me she was going to take a shower and I could do the same if I wanted. She said I could put the bill on her card. By the time we climbed back into the truck, the sun was coming up. I didn't know exactly where we were, but I knew it was somewhere in New Mexico.

The woman climbed behind the wheel, and I crawled into the sleeper. I did not know how long I had slept. When I awoke, the truck was parked alongside a two-lane highway. I looked out of the passenger's side window, then crawled over the console and looked out the driver's side. The land was flat, and I could see for miles. I didn't see the woman anywhere. The key was left in the ignition. I turned it over, and the truck started up. Seconds later, the driver's door flew open. The woman looked at me and asked what the hell I was doing. I explained to her I didn't see her and just wondered if the truck had broken down. She told me we were broken down, but it wasn't the engine. The back axel had come loose. She said she had already called for help, but it would be at least six hours before anyone could get to us. Traffic was slow; only a few cars had passed. None of the people inside them seemed interested in stopping to help.

I crawled under the trailer and looked for myself. The woman was right in a sense. The axel was loose, but the bolts were still in place. I tightened them the best I could with my hand but knew I needed a wrench to finish the job. The woman said she didn't carry a toolbox because she knew nothing when it came to fixing.

I saw a pickup coming toward us. I stood in the middle of the highway, waving my arms above my head. The pickup truck came to a stop about twenty yards in front of me. Two Mexican men, I guessed to be in their late twenties, stepped out. Both were holding pistols at my chest. The woman spoke to them in Spanish, which seemed to work because they lowered their pistols.

One of the men reached into the back of their pickup and brought out a toolbox. He walked past me without speaking, then crawled under the trailer. The other man stood holding onto his pistol. I turned around and climbed up into the semi's driver seat. I reached across and got the pistol I had placed inside the tote bag. Ten minutes later, the man crawled from under the trailer. He said something in Spanish. He smiled when the woman reached into her pocket and pulled out a wad of hundred-dollar bills. It was what he did next that gave me another life-changing choice: fight or flight. I chose to fight.

The Mexican pulled his pistol from behind his back and shot the woman in her head. I really didn't have time to think. The man was raising his arm. Before he was able to level his pistol on me, I stuck my own pistol out the window and shot him. I saw the other man turn toward their pickup. I fired three shots, one of them hitting him in the back of his head. I jumped out of the rig and checked on the woman. There wasn't anything I could do for her. The bullet had entered her forehead and exited the back leaving parts of her brain lying on the highway. I still don't know what made me do what I did next. I walked over to the man who had shot her and put two bullets in his head.

I crawled under the trailer to check the man's work. I saw where instead of fixing it, he had taken it apart. I was afraid and angry, but more angry than scared. I went through the men's pockets; neither of them had a dime. I picked up their pistols, lay them in their pickup seat, and then climbed back up into the rig. I threw my tote bag out on the ground, then wiped every place I believed I had touched with a rag. I even wiped areas I knew I hadn't touched before climbing down to the highway. Finally, I looked down at the dead woman. I told her I was sorry I had to leave her that way, then got into the Mexican's pickup and drove away.

I had driven at least ten miles before I met a car traveling in the direction of the big rig. I lowered my head as it passed, not wanting the driver to see my face. About ten miles later, I drove into a town. I couldn't pronounce the name. I stopped at a service station, filled up with gas, and asked for directions to the nearest interstate. Twenty miles later, I pulled onto I-10 somewhere in west New Mexico.

I drove on for another day and night, stopping every now and again for food and gas. I drove on to Phoenix, Arizona. I rented a motel room, slept for twelve hours, took a shower, changed my clothes, and then drove to Yuma. I pulled into the parking lot of a Gray Dog bus station, wiped the pickup down, then caught a bus to San Diego. There was a map of the city hanging on the wall inside the bus station. My heart raced, and my breathing became almost impossible when I placed my finger on the man's address.

From where I stood, it couldn't be more than two miles away. Instead of taking a cab, I chose to walk. The address I had memorized turned out to be a five-story apartment building. The apartment number was 321. I tried to control my breathing as I walked up the three flights of stairs. Once I stood in front of the door with 321 above it, I pulled the pistol from under my shirt. I was prepared to kick the door open, but I found it unlocked when I tried the knob. I shoved it open and stepped inside. In that very instant, I knew I was in the right apartment, and there was no doubt this man was responsible for the death of my wife and son. The gun that was missing from my top dresser drawer lay on a table beside the couch.

A door to my left swung open. I spun around, pointing the pistol in my hand in its direction. From the look on the man's face, I knew he recognized me and knew my intentions. He caught me off guard when he bolted straight for me. I took a step backward, falling over a chair. I rolled to my side, aiming the pistol in his direction. Before I could pull the trigger, he ran out onto the balcony. I got to my feet and out onto the balcony to see the man fall to his death. He attempted to jump from his own balcony to his neighbor's. His attempt failed. He landed on the sidewalk below.

I could see people gathering around him. Some of them looked up at me. By the time I walked back down the stairs, the police were already there. It was when they pulled their weapons, pointing them in my direction, I realized I still had the pistol in my hand. The truth is, thinking back to that very moment, I wish I had raised my arm instead of dropping that pistol on the ground.

Now, here I sit on Alabama's death row, talking to a priest. California law could only hold me for illegal possession of a firearm. I had purposely killed the two Mexican men, and no one cared. Twelve Alabama jurors convicted me of killing the old woman who shot herself. Seriously, can you believe this mess? I watched as the priest looked at his watch and made the sign of the cross. I knew then the time had come to count minutes.

DARK SPIRITS

CHAPTER 11

Clark looked across the bay and saw the monsters dancing around the fire. His telescope brought them into his bedroom. His mother told him there were no such things, but now he knew better.

At the age of ten, Clark Carter wanted to be the smartest kid on earth. He read every book he could get his hands on. The book, titled <u>Dark Spirits,</u> opened his eyes to a world most people refused to believe existed. The book described dark spirits as the evil ones who could enter into weak-minded people, causing them to do things society considered criminal. Now, every time Clark listened to the news on his television or read stories in the paper, he knew why people did the things they did.

The following day, while eating breakfast, Clark listened to his mother and father talk about a man who kidnapped young women and used them for his pleasure. Clark wondered if he *could speak* with the man and explain to him why he abducted women. Clark thought *if I tell the man what I know, maybe the man would stop.* His mother and father continued to talk on the subject.

"Mark my words. They are going to find him here." Clark's father said to his mother.

"They have every law enforcement officer in the state looking for that." Looking over at Clark, his father stopped talking in mid-sentence, placed his fork on his plate, and said, "Well, they are going to find him."

Clark's mother nodded. Clark excused himself from the table and finished getting ready for the day. His parents continued their morning discussion without his presence.

Putting on his backpack as he was going out the door, Clark called out to his mother as she was sweeping the floor and watching her husband back their car out of the driveway, "I'll be late coming home. I have to go to the library." It wasn't unusual for him to stay at the library until it closed. In fact, his mother had to get the police to let Clark out on two occasions when he had been overlooked and locked inside.

He walked to the nearest bus stop and boarded the southbound to Harbor Street. People called this the town's armpit because most of the people who hung out there were drug addicts, prostitutes, or sex freaks. Clark had seen the man's picture in the newspaper and knew exactly what he looked like. His next mission would be finding him.

Around seven p.m., Clark saw a man who fitted the description. He had the same height, build, and the same ugly scar on his left cheek. Clark knew he would have to be careful. His own life depended on it. He stayed across the street, watching the man and a woman, debating whether he should just walk over and talk to him. He saw them get into the cab of an old truck. He eased his way up behind the truck and climbed on the back. He had just settled himself under an old tarp when the truck started rolling. He had never been this afraid in his life. He didn't know what he would have to do, but he did know his mission had changed. Now he needed to save the young woman.

The truck stopped. Clark heard the woman arguing with the man. The truck door opened, then closed. He crawled from underneath the tarp and peered over the side of the bed. He could see the woman struggling. The man seemed to be dragging her toward an old house. *Now, what do I do?* Clark thought.

As soon as the man and woman were inside the house, Clark climbed out of the truck. He walked to the side of the old house. Clark saw a milk crate, picked it up, placed it beneath a window, and stepped up to look inside. He watched as the man tied the woman to a chair before leaving the room. Clark didn't hesitate. Opening the window, he crawled inside and ran over to the woman. Clark saw the fear in her eyes. He covered the woman's mouth with his tiny hand. "Don't say anything. I'm here to help you," he whispered. The woman nodded her head. He untied her hands and feet, helped her through the window, and followed behind her.

They were both on the ground, moving away from the house when the front door opened. The man ran out. "Stop!" he yelled.

Clark grabbed the woman's hand, pulling her toward a wooded area. "Run!" he cried. Looking over his shoulder, Clark saw that the man was not far behind. Letting go of the woman's hand, he spoke to her, "No matter what happens, keep running."

Clark turned and quickly ducked to hide behind the tree in front of him. He picked up the largest stick he could find. When the man ran by, Clark stepped out, hit the man on his legs, then ran. The woman had stopped, waiting for him. They could hear the man yelling something about killing them both. They ran until they were sure they had gotten away from the man, and stopped to catch their breath.

As they walked down the dark dirt road, it was Clark who broke their silence. "It wasn't him," he said.

The woman looked at the boy puzzled, "What do you mean, it wasn't him?" she asked.

Clark explained to her about the Dark Spirits. "They're out there, you know. I've been studying what makes people do bad things. There is another life form out there. It's what makes people do the things they do. I don't know where they come from. I only know they exist," he said.

The woman stopped and looked down at him. "Look, kid. I don't know what the hell you are talking about. What I do know is that man attacked me. He lied. He said he had a sick mother, and he would give me three hundred dollars if I would help him bathe her. I needed the money, so I went with him. As you can see, turns out he is some kind of monster," she said.

Clark stomped his foot on the ground. "That's what I have been trying to tell you. It was a monster, not the man. He has a Dark Spirit inside him. And, by the way, my name is not 'kid'. It's Clark."

"For the record, kid, uh… Clark. My name is Dawn, and all this crap you're saying doesn't make sense to me. And the truth is, I really don't want to hear it. All I want to do is find a phone and call the police."

The density of the woods compounded the darkness. They could barely see. Clark didn't know how long they had been walking when he saw the light, and he realized it came from the front porch of a house. The house stopped them in their tracks. They must have walked in a circle; the man's place was right in front of them again.

Dawn started to cry. "What the hell are we going to do now?"

Clark thought for a few minutes before he answered. "Can you drive?"

"Yes," Dawn said.

"I read a book once about how to hotwire a car." Clark pointed towards the old truck. "I believe I can start it."

"Sounds like a plan. I'll go over by that tree and watch out for the man. You start the truck, and I'll come running," Dawn said.

Before Dawn made it to the tree, she heard the truck start. She ran over and slid into the driver's seat. Clark looked at her and smiled, "He left the keys in the truck."

Dawn put the truck into gear and started down the drive. Suddenly, the back window of the truck exploded. Tiny particles of glass flew through the cab. Dawn screamed but kept the truck moving. She saw Clark slump over in the seat. Blood covered the back of his head. A few minutes later, he raised his head and looked at her. "Are you alright?" he asked.

"Yes, but you're not. I need to get you to the hospital. You're bleeding pretty bad."

Clark reached up and touched the back of his head. "I don't think I'm shot. I just got cut by the glass. I'll be okay."

Thirty minutes later, while Clark was having the glass removed from his head, Dawn called his mother. Clark tried to tell the hospital personnel about the Dark Spirits, but no one would listen to him. He knew somehow he needed to find proof to show everyone he was right. Dawn left the hospital with the police. She intended to lead them to the man's house, but Clark knew he would no longer be there. The Dark Spirits would warn him.

The next morning, Clark's thoughts were confirmed. The news anchor said the man had fled before the police arrived. Clark knew the Dark Spirits would strike again, and once more, he wanted to stop them. A new destination entered his mind.

A little before midnight, Clark exited the bus. This time he decided on a different part of town, where people had the same characteristics as the others: drug addicts, prostitutes, sex freaks, all the same. The difference between these people and the ones on Harbor Street was their wealth. Fancy cars, fancy bags, fancy clothes, but still a good place for the Dark Spirits to continue their quest.

Clark smiled to himself when he realized his hunch turned out to be right on target. The same man with the scar on his left cheek exited from a car directly across from where he stood. Clark saw the man engage in a conversation with another young woman. He pulled his cell phone out of his pocket and dialed 911. He told the police where they could find the man who kidnapped the woman.

He saw the man take ahold of the woman's arm as he walked toward his car. Afraid the police wouldn't get there in time, Clark decided to stop him. He ran across the street, waving his arms in the air.

"Hey, mister! Stop. It's not you doing this. They have you," he yelled. The man and woman stopped. Clark was close enough to see the woman's confused face and the anger in the man's eyes. "Run, lady," Clark said. The man looked up and down the street. Police cars came from both directions. He looked down at Clark.

"Who the hell are you?" he asked.

"I'm just trying to help you, mister," Clark said. The man didn't put up a fight. Dropping to his knees, the man placed his hands on his head as if he knew the drill.

Clark tried to tell the police about the Dark Spirits, but once again, no one listened. After sitting in the police station for a while, as they booked the man with the scar, they called Clark's mother. His mom drove him home in silence. Once they made it home, she told him to go straight to his room, and he wasn't to come out until she called for him. She needed to calm down. His father was out of town for business, but she needed him as she thought of Clark. A phone call would have to do.

The next morning, Clark sat on his side of his bed. He heard his mother's footsteps as she came up the stairs. He looked up as she entered his room.

"What's wrong with you?" she asked

. "The only thing wrong, Mother, is no one will believe me. I have discovered the truth about why people do bad things. The Dark Spirits are here and have been for a long time. I can't explain why, but now they want people to know they are here. I read where sometime in the 1950's they introduced people to the television... and look at our electronics today. At the push of a button, we can see all the way around the world. They want us to know every violent crime is being committed by them and not the people. I led the police to the man who kidnapped those women. I wanted to prove the Dark Spirits were leading him. If you call the police now, they will tell you the man doesn't remember what he did or why. The Dark Spirits have left him. It's because he is locked up, so they have no further use for him. But I assure you, Mother, somewhere tonight, someone else will kidnap and murder another poor woman. You have to believe me," he said.

Clark's mother left the room. A few minutes later, she returned. "I have found someone willing to listen to your story about those spirits. We will leave as soon as you get dressed."

Three days later, Clark looked out the window. He no longer had his telescope and could only peer through the bars that held him captive. He turned around as the door opened, and an older woman walked into the room. He walked over and sat on the edge of his bed. The woman sat in a chair beside him.

The woman stared at a clipboard for a few minutes before she spoke.

"How is it that only you can see the Dark Spirits?" she asked.

Clark couldn't believe what he had just heard. She was the first person besides himself to actually say the words 'Dark Spirits,' so he thought maybe she did believe him. He sat up straight and looked into her eyes.

"They dance on the beach behind my house."

"How many of these 'Dark Spirits' have you seen?"

"I don't know how many, but I see them every night. One night, I went down to the beach, and I hid behind a fire barrel. One of them saw me and came over to talk."

"And what did he say?" the woman asked.

"It was a she," Clark said.

"Okay, what did she say?" the woman asked.

"She said, and I read it in a book too, when we die, we change into a spirit. Some are good, and some are bad. The good ones are called Light, and the bad ones are called Dark. How you live, and your life's actions determine your lightness and your darkness as a spirit. Sometimes, the Dark Spirits take over good people and make them do bad things. And when the people get locked up, the Dark Spirits leave their body."

"So, you're telling me, you believe every bad deed is committed by someone possessed by one of these spirits?"

"Yes," Clark said.

The woman stood up. She looked down at Clark. "You believe once people get locked up, they are left without a spirit," she said.

Clark shook his head. "No, we all have a spirit, but you see, some of us can control our spirit, and some of us can't," he said.

The woman smiled and touched Clark on top of his head. "What kind of spirit do I have?" she asked.

Clark saw the gleam in the woman's eyes. He jumped up and ran through the door. The hallway was empty. He ran toward a door at the far end of the hall. With every step, the door moved farther and farther away. He tripped and fell. The floor moved from beneath him. Falling with his eyes closed, he screamed as he fell through the emptiness of air. Feeling the freedom and the loss of being grounded, he opened his eyes. He found himself in his own home, inside his bedroom, and lying on his bed. His mother stood over him. "Wake up, Clark. You are having another bad dream."

Only Clark knew this was no bad dream. The Dark Spirits were real, and now he would give them proof. Clark felt the knife under his pillow, and the coldness caressed his hands. He looked up at his mother and smiled.

THE E VIRUS

CHAPTER 12

Although I didn't know where they came from, I could see three of them from where I stood. The sun was going down behind the trees. They all stood on the second rail of our fence. I could see their faces clearly. The tall blonde girl had a nose that seemed too big for her face, but this didn't matter. I still thought her pretty. The black-haired girl was short and kind of fat. The boy had red or maybe brown hair. I couldn't really tell with the sun shining behind him, but I thought him younger than the girls.

I didn't know if they had seen me. I ducked inside the barn. I watched from a knothole in the wall as they came over the fence. The three of them walked forward. Mother was in there alone. I knew I had to stop them. They were halfway between me and the house when I stepped out of the barn.

It was the boy who saw me. He said something to the girls. I don't know why, but it seemed like my breath stopped when the girls turned and looked at me. I took a moment to calm my fears, then walked toward them. They stood still. Neither of them spoke until I was within a few feet from them.

It was the boy who spoke. He said the three of them were lost. They had been walking for days and needed food and water. I could tell by the looks on their faces he was telling me the truth. My fears had gone. I actually felt sorry for them.

I told them to go to the barn. In the second stall, they would find a sack of sweet potatoes, and they could take as many as they wanted. I told them it would be dark soon. They could stay the night inside the barn. I told them I would go to the house and bring back bread, water, and blankets. Without another word, I walked away from the barn.

"Who are they?" Mother asked as I walked into the house.

"I don't know, Mother. They have been walking for days. They are tired and hungry. I'm going to feed them and let them spend the night in our barn. You get some sleep. I will tell you more when I come in."

Her face questioned me before she stated, "Allen, are you going to…."

"No, Mother, they mean us no harm."

"Are you sure?" she asked. "You know what happened last time."

"Yes, Mother, how could I forget."

I filled a jug with water and took two loaves of bread from the table. The blankets were in the shed behind our house. I could come back for them. I thought back on my mother's question.

Are you sure? I really wasn't sure, but I hoped they were different. It had been almost one year since anyone had been here. The last two my mother referred to were a man and woman. They seemed fine at first, but Mother heard the man tell the woman he had the fever. Mother shot them both. I had put on my gloves and mask, tied them behind the tractor with a rope, drug them behind the north pasture, dug a deep hole, and buried them next to the others.

Now there were three people inside our barn. We were told the virus started with a fever. I would have to touch them all to be sure.

***

Josh Odell stood at the top of the stairs. His eighteen-year-old daughter, Leah, and sixteen-year-old son, Peter, stood at the bottom, looking up at him. Both had tears running down their faces.

"I don't have a choice. I have to go," Josh said.

"When are you coming back?" Leah asked.

Josh walked down the stairs. He sat down on the second step, then reached out and took Leah's hand.

"You know I can't answer that question. We don't know how many are sick, but we do want to save as many as we can."

"But, Dad, there are a lot of sick people here in Alabama. Why do you have to go all the way to Texas?" Peter asked.

"There are enough doctors here. I'm going to a small town called Dewsome, where there is only one doctor. He sent word he needed my help and also needed more supplies," Josh said.

"I still don't like it," Leah said. Josh stood up.

"Look, you two. I don't know the exact day, but let me promise you this: I will be back here soon." He hugged both Leah and Peter, then walked out the door.

Leah stood on the second floor of their home in Clio, Alabama, looking out of her bedroom window. It had been nine days since her father had left for Texas and two days since her brother had left for who knows where. Twice, someone had tried to break into their house, but Leah had frightened them away with a recording of a barking dog. Now, she may have to do it again, but maybe not. The girl who stood at the end of their drive was tall with long blonde hair, but looked no older than Leah herself. She looked up at the window, then walked on down the street. Leah raised her bedroom window.

"Hey, wait!" she yelled. The girl turned around and looked up. "Are you alright?" Leah asked.

Without speaking, the girl walked toward the house. Leah closed the window, ran down the stairs, and opened the front door. The girl stood on the porch in front of her.

"I could use some food," she said.

"Are you sick?" Leah asked. The girl tilted her head.

"Do you have the virus?" Leah asked.

"Oh, no, no. I've been staying in an old house down by the river ever since this thing started. I ran out of food two days ago. How about you?" the girl asked.

"No, I'm fine. I haven't left this house in months. Come in. I have food," Leah said.

"We have soup and lots of it, but not many varieties. We have beef, chicken, and beans, and franks."

Without giving the girl time to make her request, Leah took two cans of beef soup off the shelf.

"What's your name?" Leah asked.

"It's Ragan Till."

"Where are you from?" Leah asked as she poured the soup into a pot and set it on the stove.

"Montgomery, but when the virus started, we moved out to the country. My brother got sick, so my father took him back to town. By the time he got back, my mother was sick. He gave me some money, put me in a boat, and sent me downriver to one of his friends' houses. When I got there, no one was home, and no one ever showed up. Like I said, I ran out of food two days ago, so I started walking. I haven't seen anyone else until you yelled at me," she said. Leah poured the soup into two bowls. She handed one to Ragan.

"You can stay here if you want," Leah said.

***

Peter walked up the back steps. When he turned the knob, the door was locked. He started banging on it with his hand.

"Leah, let me in!" he yelled. Moments later, the door swung open.

"Peter, where the hell have you been?" Leah asked.

Peter rushed past her. "Quick! Close the door! People are chasing me."

"Who are they?" Leah asked.

"I have no idea who they are, but they're shooting everyone on sight. They're going from house to house, setting them on fire. We don't have much time, so we need to go now."

"Where are we going?" Ragan asked.

Peter spun around. "Who are you?"

"Peter, this is Ragan. Don't ask any questions. She's coming with us. Now, go upstairs and get our backpacks. Make sure to Look in dad's closet; there is another one in there. We will take as much food and water as the three of us can carry," Leah said.

"You still haven't answered my question. Where are we going?" Ragan asked.

Leah grabbed six plastic bottles from under the sink. "Here, fill these with water. We can figure out where to go once we get started," she said.

Twenty minutes later, the three of them stood in the backyard. Leah looked at Ragan. "How far is it to the old house where you were staying?" she asked.

"It's not far, but the people might come there, too," Ragan said.

"I know, but I thought maybe we could use your boat. We could go downriver, deeper into the country where no one would look for us. Once we are out of harm's way, we can decide what to do next," Leah said.

"Sounds like a good plan to me. Lead the way," Peter said.

One hour later, Leah and Ragan watched as Peter loaded the three backpacks into the boat

"I thought it would be much bigger," Leah said.

Peter looked over his shoulder. "Yeah, and I thought it would at least have a motor," he said.

"It did have a motor when I left it here. Let's be thankful that who-ever took it, didn't take the paddles," Ragan said.

"Yeah, you're right. Let's get going," Peter said. He waited until the girls were settled, then got into the boat and pushed away from the shore.

Leah saw the smoke from the burning house. "Looks like some of those people have already been through here," she said.

Peter held up his hand. "Be quiet. I see some of them beside the house over there," he said, pointing his finger in their direction. The three of them sat still. No one spoke as the small boat drifted down the river.

Ragan reached down, picked up one of the paddles, and handed it to Leah. She dipped the end of the other paddle into the water. "I believe we are safe now. Come on, help me paddle. We need to get as far away as we can... and fast," Ragan said.

Paddling and thinking, Leah came up with a plan, but she knew it wouldn't work when she saw the dam up ahead.

"What do we do now?" Peter asked.

Leah looked over toward the shore, then back at her brother. "We can stay in the woods for tonight. Tomorrow we will walk southwest toward the ocean. When we get there, we can steal a boat and go to Texas. We need to find dad."

"You do know it's over a hundred miles to the ocean from here, don't you?" Ragan asked.

"Do you have a better idea?" Leah said.

"No, I guess not," Ragan said.

"Then, it's a plan."

Leah didn't know if she was bolted awake by Peter's scream or by the pain in her side from where the man had kicked her; she opened her eyes and noticed two men standing over her. She saw another man holding Peter's hair in one hand, and a large knife in the other. Ragan was nowhere in sight. Before she could say anything, she heard two loud pops, then a few seconds later, another pop. The man holding Peter's hair had let Peter go. He dropped the knife and fell to the ground. Leah realized the other two were already dead.

Ragan walked out from the bushes holding a revolver in her hand. "Are you alright?' she asked Leah.

"Yeah, I think so. Where the hell did you get that gun?"

"I've had it with me the whole time. I found it inside the old house I was staying in."

"Where did you learn to shoot like that?" Peter asked.

"I didn't know I could. I woke up and needed to relieve myself. I was over there behind those bushes. I heard the men talking. I stood still, hoping they would walk on by, but one of them spotted the two of you. I was just going to try and scare them away with the gun, then that man kicked you, so I just started pulling the trigger. Lucky shots, I guess."

"Yeah, lucky for us. And thank you," Leah said.

Peter rolled one of the dead men over on his back.

"What are you doing?" Leah asked.

"I'm checking for cash. We might need it somewhere down the road. You know, we really don't know what's ahead of us." He came up with two hundred and fifty dollars. He held it up and smiled. "Where to now?" he asked.

Ragan pointed toward two tall pine trees. "Those men came from over there. They might have left a car or truck somewhere close by."

"Can you drive?" Leah asked.

"Yeah, I'm seventeen. I got my license last year," Ragan said.

The path they took led them to a dirt road. There wasn't a car or truck in sight. They walked down the dirt road until they came to a place where it crossed a highway. They hid behind some trees and watched several cars go by, followed by what looked like two Army trucks. One of the trucks had men riding on the back of it.

"Do you think if we were to stop one of those trucks, they would help us?" Ragan asked.

"No, those are the people who are burning the houses. I think they would kill us," Peter said.

"So, where do we go now?" Ragan asked.

Leah stepped out from behind the trees and glanced up and down the highway. "We could follow the trucks." Ragan walked up beside her. "I agree. If we stay as far as we can behind them, we should be safe," she said.

Peter looked up at the sun. "It's the wrong way."

"What are you talking about?" Leah asked.

Peter looked at his sister, "You said we were going to the ocean, steal a boat, and find dad. Those trucks are traveling east, and the ocean is south. It's the wrong way."

"So, what do you think we should do?" Ragan asked.

Peter looked up at the sky and observed their surroundings, "I think we should go back into the woods until it gets dark, then make our way around the dam, find another boat, and follow the river. It should take us to the ocean."

Not secure with Peter's thought, Ragan spoke her mind. "I still think we should follow the trucks."

"No, no. Peter is right. We should hide in the woods until dark. Travel downriver at night. If we run into anyone who means us harm, we have your gun," Leah said.

"What if we can't find a boat?" Ragan said.

"Then we walk," Peter said.

That night, they stayed in the woods but followed the highway toward the dam. They came to another road, crossing the one they followed. Peter raised his hand, motioning for the girls to stop. He couldn't believe their luck. Sitting right in front of them sat a Ford pickup truck with a boat and trailer hooked onto it. He looked over at the girls. "You two stay here while I check it out."

Leah grabbed his arm; he was her little brother. She didn't want anything happening to him. He turned and looked into her eyes, and her inner thoughts said, *let him go.* "Be careful," she said.

Peter walked to the edge of the highway. He stood looking and listening but didn't see or hear anyone. Peter was afraid, but his male ego didn't want the girls to know. He took a deep breath, then walked up to the truck. Looking in through the driver's side window, he immediately turned away and threw up. A man lay across the seat with half of his face missing. As soon as he was able to straighten up, he noticed the girls coming toward him.

"Stop! I told you to wait." To his surprise, both girls stopped in their tracks. He walked around to the passenger's side and opened the door. He saw the keys dangling from the ignition. He pulled the man out of the truck, dragging him down an embankment, out of sight from the highway. Using his shirt, Peter wiped chunks of meat and blood off of the truck seat; he reached over and turned the key. The engine turned over a few times, then started. He looked back to where Leah and Ragan stood.

"Let's roll!" he yelled.

Ragan got in behind the wheel, Leah sat next to her, and Peter sat next to the window.

"Where to?" Ragan asked.

"From what I see, we have two choices. We could try and cross the dam, hoping there's no one on it, or I see a dirt road about twenty yards on down which should take us back to the river," Peter said.

"We do have another choice. We could unhook the boat and just follow the highway," Leah said.

"We can't. I think we should take the dirt road, and soon," Ragan said.

Leah looked over at her. "Why can't we take the highway?"

Ragan put the truck in gear and drove toward the dirt road. "Because this truck is almost out of gas," she said.

A couple of miles from where they started, the river's edge came into view. Peter watched out the window looking for an ideal location.

"Stop!" he yelled a little louder than he intended. Ragan stomped on the brakes, causing them to rock forward.

"Sorry, I didn't mean to yell. But I believe you can back the boat into the water over there," Peter said, pointing toward the river. Ragan put the truck in park. The three of them walked down to the river's edge.

"What do you think?" Leah asked.

Ragan looked back up at the boat. "The water is too deep. The trailer will sink, but I think I know a way."

They walked back up to the boat. Ragan looked at Peter. "See if there is a rope inside the boat," she said.

Peter stepped up on the trailer, then looked into the boat. He gave the thumbs up.

"Okay, here is what we need to do. Tie the rope to a tree, then loosen the latch connecting the trailer to the truck. I believe there is enough of a downhill grade. We can all jump up and down on the truck's bumper. The trailer will come loose and then roll into the water. The trailer will sink, but we can use the rope and pull the boat close enough to the shore for us to get inside," Ragan said.

Twenty minutes later, Ragan showed Leah how to put the boat in reverse, then went to the back of the boat. "I'm going to prime the motor. When I tell you to, turn the key, okay, Leah?" Leah nodded.

Peter threw their backpacks into the boat. "Do you want me to untie the rope?" he asked.

Ragan held up her hand. "Not yet. Wait until we get the motor started." A few seconds later, Ragan stood up and looked at Leah. "Now!" she yelled. The motor roared to life. "Yes!" Leah yelled.

Peter untied the rope then climbed into the boat. Ragan moved up beside Leah. "Okay, now pull the lever down into reverse. Once we are far enough away from the shore, pull it down into low gear," she pointed to another lever. "This is the gas. The further forward you push it, the faster we will go. Once we start moving forward, pull the gear lever down into high. Then, use the steering wheel and guide us anywhere you want to go," she said.

Peter moved up beside Leah and Ragan. "It's getting daylight. We need to stick to our plan," he said.

Ragan stood up and looked downriver. "He's right- pullover closer to the shore. We can find a slew, pull the boat out of sight, and rest until dark," she said.

Leah opened her eyes. She lay on her back, looking up at the stars with Ragan beside her on the boat's bottom. Peter slept sitting in the driver's seat. Trying not to disturb them, Leah climbed out of the boat. She needed to relieve herself. Her intentions went to no avail. Both Peter and Ragan raised up and looked at her.

"Where are you going?" Peter asked. "I've got to go... you know," she said.

"Yeah, me too!" he said.

"Wait for me!" Ragan said.

Peter built a small fire. "What are you doing? We need to go," Leah said.

Peter reached into the boat and pulled out one of the backpacks. "Do you realize we haven't eaten in over twenty-four hours? We need to eat," he said.

"Come to think of it, I'm starved," Leah said.

Finished eating and back in the boat, Ragan guided them to the middle of the river. She pushed the gas lever as far forward as it would go. The boat glided across the water. Once she believed the boat couldn't go any faster, she reached down and cut the engine. Both Leah and Peter looked at her. "The speed of the boat and the river's current should push us at least a couple of miles down the river. Not only are we saving gas, but we also cut down on the risk of someone hearing us," she said.

Ragan repeated the procedure several times, pushing them further down the river. The first night seemed to go by fast. The second night even faster. It was on the third night they encountered more people. The boat drifted quietly around a bend. Before Ragan could react, the other boat was upon them. It passed by at a high rate of speed. It made a wide sweep on the river, turning back in their direction. Ragan pulled the revolver from her coat pocket, pointed it toward the other boat, and pulled the trigger twice. To their surprise and relief, the other boat made another broad sweep and turned away from them. Suddenly, the motor to their boat sputtered. Realizing what was happening, Ragan turned the boat toward the shore.

"What's going on?" Leah asked.

"As far as the other boat, I don't know. As far as this boat, we are running out of gas," Ragan said.

"Isn't there enough to give us at least one more good run?" Peter asked.

"Yes, but we don't know what those other people will do. We need to get out of sight for now," Ragan said.

Ragan saw a small slew ahead of them. "We can hide in there, but I believe from now on, we are on foot." As if on cue, the boat motor sputtered and died. She guided them through the narrow path, allowing the boat to ground itself.

Peter threw the backpack on the ground, then climbed out of the boat. He looked back at Leah. "I have to go," he said.

Leah laughed, "What are you telling me for? Go."

"No, you don't understand. I feel sick. I think I have the virus. I need to go so the two of you won't get it," Peter said.

"We haven't been around anyone with the virus. There's no way you could have it," Leah said.

"I think I might have been around someone when we found the truck. I pulled a dead man out of it. He had been shot, but he could have had the virus."

Ragan stepped down off of the boat. "Look, Peter, you just said you feel sick. It could be from lack of food or rest. Let's go further into these woods. We can eat and get some sleep and then see how you feel," she said.

Leah awoke to the sound of laughter. The sun was shining on her face. "What in the world is going on?" she asked.

Ragan and Peter stood beside a small fire. Both had stripped down to their underwear. "It was ticks," Ragan said.

Leah tilted her head. "Ticks?" she asked.

"Think, Leah. Even though we have been on this river for days, when is the last time you bathed yourself? We are covered in ticks. I believe it's why Peter felt sick. I found five on him. He found seven on me. Come on, take off your clothes. I'll check you over, then we all need to go down to the river and bathe," Ragan said.

Ragan found two ticks on Leah- one in her hair and the other stuck to the back of her leg. After bathing and checking their clothes, once again, they were on their way on foot.

The sun was going down. It had been three days since they had left the river.

"We need to find a place and stop for the night," Peter said.

"Let's keep going. We are out of food. Maybe we can at least find some water up ahead," Leah said.

They walked up a steep hill, then down, then down the other side. Peter was the first to see the smoke coming from a smokestack on top of an old house. He stepped up on the second rail of a wooden fence. Leah and Ragan climbed up beside him.

"What do you think?" Leah asked. "I think we should knock on the door and ask for some food," Peter said.

"Yeah, let's go," Ragan said.

Halfway between the fence and the house, Peter saw the man come out of the barn.

"Stop. There's a man over there by the barn," he said.

"He's coming toward us," Ragan said.

"Just stay calm. He's not carrying a gun. I think we will be okay," Peter said.

When the man walked up to them, Peter realized he wasn't much older than any of them.

"Hi. We're lost. We have been walking for days. We could use some food and water," Peter said.

The man looked back and forth from Ragan to Leah.

"Go down to the barn. In the second stall, you will find a sack of sweet potatoes. Take as many as you need. It's getting dark. Stay in our barn for the night. I'll go up to the house and bring back some bread, water, and blankets."

The young man turned and walked toward his house without saying another word.

***

When I got back to the house, Mother was still awake. She wanted to know if any of the people had the virus. I told her I thought the boy could have, but it didn't matter. I'd already taken care of them. Mother looked me in my eyes. "Allen, you didn't hurt those young people, did you?"

"Of course not, Mother," I lied.

***

They called it the E. virus; it came from across the pond. Some doctor brought it over here, and it spread faster than expected. Realizing it couldn't be detained, the government decided to take out everyone who could have come in contact with the virus. They came here. Mother and I hid in the woods; it was raining, so they didn't burn our home. Mother and I live in fear. I'm not a bad guy. I just do what I have to do for our protection and pray for the day this will all end.

THE TRAP

CHAPTER 13

"Why would you do a thing like that?"

"It was your suggestion. Why are you questioning the outcome?"

"I didn't think this one through."

"Stop it. This makes nine times. Isn't it obvious that those things are not going to let anyone else see them?"

"I keep thinking about Max."

"You shouldn't. It was Max's ego that cost him his life. And, there is no way you should believe what happened this time was your fault."

"Let's not talk about this now. We have more important issues to discuss."

"No, we don't. Let's finish this conversation. Did you read the morning paper?"

"No, should I have?"

"It won't be necessary. I will read it to you."

"I figured you might. First, let me get a cup of coffee."

Dr. Kenneth Moon smiled to himself as he turned his back to his protege. As he poured coffee into a cup, he could hear her unfolding the newspaper. *So, it didn't even make the front page,* he thought to himself. He knew today things would be in his favor. He would no longer be directly involved, and she would unknowingly take over his quest. At his present age, he knew the time had come for his return.

Brenda Carson had personal experiences regarding Dr. Moon's teachings of an underworld. In her mind, he was more than a teacher; Dr. Moon was also her friend. Carson, age thirty, and Moon, age sixty, were decades apart in cultural events, but when it came to the underworld, Brenda's thoughts matched his. She cleared her throat and began to read.

"Another tragic accident in the desert outside San Diego. As of yet, it is not known how many lives were lost. The students were attempting to enter a large sinkhole under the assumption of finding life inside the underworld when the hole closed up around them. They were following the teachings of Dr. Kenneth Moon, who has not been available for comment. Crews have been digging day and night to no avail. Not one body has been found. Authorities are in the courts trying to stop future projects."

"Maybe they're right," Dr. Moon said.

"About what?" Brenda asked.

Brenda folded the paper and lay it on the table. "We can't stop now. It wouldn't be fair to Max. It was you and I who told him. He believed us and died trying to prove to the world what you and I know is true," she said.

Dr. Moon stood up from the table. "Do you know it's true?" he asked. Brenda stood up, walked around the table, and stood in front of him. She reached out and put both hands on his shoulders.

"Do you really want me to answer that question?" she said.

TWO YEARS EARLIER

Maxwell Culverhouse, a.k.a. Max, stood looking down into the sinkhole. It appeared overnight in a field behind his home in San Diego, California. As far as he knew, no one else had discovered this strange phenomenon. He walked back to where he had parked his truck, picked up his phone, and punched in the number to the only person he believed would explain it.

Dr. Kenneth Moon sat next to a window watching the people walk by on a busy sidewalk in New York while eating his lunch. His phone vibrated inside his shirt pocket. When he took it out and saw who the call was from, he smiled. "Max, what's up, my friend?" he asked.

"Are you sitting down?" Max asked.

"Yes, I'm eating my lunch," Dr. Moon said.

"Lunch? At this hour? Oh. I'm sorry. I forgot the time difference. It's still early here in San Diego," Max said.

"Now that we have the time zone figured out, what is it you wish to talk about?" Dr. Moon asked.

Max let the tailgate down on his truck and sat down. "Do you remember teaching about unexplained phenomena? You and one of your proteges had examined one, but your belief was it would never recreate itself. So what I am getting at here, Dr. Moon, is that you said this phenomenon started with a sinkhole," Max said.

"You're telling me you have found a sinkhole," Dr. Moon said.

"Yes, I have. Last night I heard strange noises in the field behind my house. I played it off as a quake, but I could feel small vibrations. As soon as day broke with enough light, I got in my truck and drove across the field. Right now, as we speak, I am looking at the hole. My guess is it's at least fifty feet in diameter. I can't guess how deep. I'm afraid to get too close to the edge," Max said.

Dr. Moon waved to the waitress and asked for his check. Before she could return, he laid a one-hundred-dollar bill on the table and walked out onto the sidewalk. "Look, Max, don't go near that hole and don't tell anyone else about it. I'm going to bring a friend. We will charter a jet and be in San Diego by three p.m. your time. I say again, Max, don't go near the hole until we get there."

After disconnecting his call, Dr. Moon punched in a number.

"Hi, Ken."

"There's another one," he said.

He knew Brenda would know precisely what he meant.

"Where?" she asked.

"San Diego."

"How did you find it?"

Dr. Moon waved his arm toward a cab. "Do you remember Maxwell Culverhouse?" he asked.

"No. Should I?" Brenda asked.

"Not really, but I thought you might. You met him once. He was one of my students at Berkeley. He just called. Said he found a sinkhole and, from the sound of it, it's twice the size of the one you and I explored. I told him to stay away and not call anyone else. I'm on my way to the airport now. I have some more calls to make. Get there as soon as you can," he said.

"I'm on my way," she said while pulling her suitcase from underneath her bed.

***

Once the jet was in the air, Brenda unbuckled her seatbelt and searched for a coffee cup. When she returned, she found Dr. Moon going through some notes on one of his tablets.

"What do you think?" he asked.

Brenda sat down beside him and took a sip of her coffee.

"If it's like the others, it should close itself within the next seventy-two hours."

"This one could take longer. Max said it could be at least fifty feet," Dr. Moon said.

"How much does this Max person know?"

Dr. Moon looked over at her and smiled. "Only what I taught him and the rest of my students."

"Then he knows nothing," Brenda said.

"I may be wrong, but it's my belief that you and I are the only people on planet earth who know these things exist," Dr. Moon said.

"Okay, we know they exist, and we know they seal themselves up, so why are we inside this jet on our way to California?"

Again, Dr. Moon looked at her and smiled. "You don't know the whole truth about these beings," he said.

"So, we are going back down and…."

"Not we, just me," Dr. Moon said before Brenda could finish her statement. "What about Maxwell?" she asked.

"I'm leaving Max with you. He's smart and will know how to operate the equipment I've ordered."

"And you are seriously thinking about going down alone?"

"Well, yes and no. I've ordered a helmet cam and radio. You and Max will be with me every step of the way."

Brenda set her coffee down on the tray beside her seat. "I see. And, this helmet cam, does it record?" she asked.

"Yes."

"You know, these beings are not dumb. I don't believe they will let themselves be recorded."

"It was me who saved the young one's life," Dr. Moon said.

"Yes, you did, and they let us live. But think of how quickly they could adapt from whatever language they were speaking and switch to speaking English. Not to mention we both know they killed people. We saw the bones, remember?"

"Yes, those bones are the reason I'm going down there alone. I couldn't live with myself if something happened to you".

"Look, Ken, I trust your ability to make sound decisions, but I believe you are making a mistake here. Even if we are successful in recording them, we couldn't show anyone without risking the lives of these beings, and for that, I couldn't live with myself," Brenda said.

"Why so much concern for them?" Dr. Moon asked.

Brenda thought for a few moments before answering her question. "I'm also concerned about the people in this world- how most believe in a God who created them. Think of what might happen to them when they find out humans, as we know them, were not the first beings on this planet," she said.

"Yes, like I've said, I thought this through, and it's the exact answer I want the world to know. It's the answer to an age-old question, which came first: the chicken or the egg?" Dr. Moon said.

"And you are willing to risk your life for this answer?" Brenda asked.

"You worry too much. I will be okay," Dr. Moon said.

The voice of the pilot came over the intercom. "Dr. Moon, we will be landing at Gillespie Field in fifteen minutes." Brenda reached down and buckled herself. She looked over at Dr. Moon. *I hope you are right about this,* she thought.

***

Brenda stepped out of the jet, and as she looked across the tarmac, she saw a pickup truck with two large crates in the truck bed. She turned and looked at Dr. Moon. "How did you arrange for this equipment to be here in such a short time?"

"I ordered it last year," Dr. Moon stated as they walked down the steps and over to the truck. Brenda asked another question, "How did you know the sinkhole would appear here in San Diego?"

Looking at Brenda, Dr. Moon was intrigued by her attention to detail. "This equipment," he stated as he touched the truck, "Was stationed in a warehouse in L.A. The first call I made after talking to you was to have these things here when we arrived."

Both of them heard, before they actually saw it, another pickup truck pulling up beside them. Maxwell Culverhouse stepped out of his vehicle and walked over, and stuck out his hand. Brenda reached out and shook it.

"Now, I remember. You're the one who believed he could build an entire city under the surface of the ocean. How did that project turn out?" she asked.

"It's good to see you again, Ms. Carson, and to answer your question, I still believe it can be done. Unfortunately, I had to abandon the project for lack of funding." Max turned and shook Dr. Moon's hand. "I appreciate you coming. As far as I know, no one else has discovered the hole. If you follow me, we can be on-site in twenty minutes," he said.

Twenty minutes later, Dr. Moon and Brenda followed Max through an open gate leading into a field. They parked their trucks twenty yards from the hole. Dr. Moon got out and looked at his watch. Four-thirty p.m. "First things first, we need to unload and set up the generator, then the table. Place the computer monitor and the recorder there, then set up the disk next to the table. I will harness myself to the winch on the front of the truck. You should be able to operate the winch from the computer so I can keep my hands free. Watch the screen closely. If you see anything before I do, let me know immediately," he said.

Max held up both hands. "Woah! Woah! Woah! If we see anything? Exactly what are we looking for?" he asked.

Dr. Moon looked at Brenda. "Tell him the truth. We have no choice but to tell him while we work. I would like to get down there before dark," he said.

Brenda took ahold of one end of a crate while Max took the other. She knew she would need to tell the story in a way Max would believe.

"Okay, listen. You will have to have an open mind here. Six years ago, Dr. Moon and I discovered one of these sinkholes outside Deming, New Mexico. We were on our way to an archaeological site where two young boys discovered the fossilized remains of a man believed to be over one thousand years old. Just for kicks and the excitement, Dr. Moon and I decided to go down into the hole and see if we could find more fossilized remains. Now, here is where you need to have an open mind. What we found wasn't fossilized nor remains...

They were live beings. About one hundred and fifty feet down, we discovered a cave. We lowered ourselves to the entrance, and using our headlamps, we walked into the dark open space. We came upon a rock slab with what looked like a child's arm sticking out from underneath it. The floor of the cave was mostly sand, so Ken- Dr. Moon- dug down with his hands until we could pull what we first thought was a human child free from underneath the rock. It was a child, but not human. Its skin was as coarse as sandpaper. It had a mouth to speak with and ears to hear, but it didn't have any eyes. It saw us with its mind. It spoke a language we couldn't understand, but as soon as Dr. Moon talked to it in English, it too could speak and understand the English language.

A few minutes later, two more of them showed up. They weren't hostile, nor did they seem as curious about us as we were about them.

I asked them questions about where they were from, but they wouldn't talk to me. Instead, they talked to Dr. Moon. I couldn't hear their conversation, but later, he told me they considered us friends because we saved their child. Also, while we were down there, the sinkhole refilled itself with sand, trapping us inside the cave.

They showed us another way out. I shined my light on the one I believed to be female. She had legs and feet like ours, except her legs were fused together. She stood on her knees, and by wiggling her feet, she moved across the sandy floor. We followed them through several chambers. In one of them, we saw human bones—thousands and thousands of them. I managed to pick up a small piece and put it inside my pocket. From my study, the bone turned out to be the little finger of a female, and it was at least one million years old.

The beings didn't come all the way to the surface, and they told Dr. Moon it wouldn't be safe for us to come back down into one of these holes, so I do hope he knows what he's doing," Brenda said.

Max looked at Dr. Moon. "Is this all true?" he asked.

"Yes, and there is more I could tell you, but it will have to wait. Right now, I need to get down there," Ken stated.

Before Dr. Ken Moon could hook himself up to his harness, the ground around them started shaking. The three of them fell to the ground. The tables collapsed, and the computer fell. Ten minutes passed before they were able to stand. The sinkhole had replaced itself with the desert sand.

"Are you guys alright?" Brenda asked.

"I think we're fine, but our hole is gone," Dr. Moon said.

Max sat back down on the ground. He looked up at Dr. Moon and Brenda. "Let's just say I have an open mind. The only evidence you have to prove your story is a finger bone that could or could not be one million years old. And let's say the only reason I believe this is because you were about to go down a hole you knew could kill you. Not to mention, there could be another reason that I don't know because you haven't told me. Now, I am going to repeat myself here. Let's say I do believe you, and I do have an open mind... what now? What do we do next?" Max stated as he caught his breath.

Dr. Moon brushed the sand from the legs of his pants. "We go home. It's over for now," he said.

Brenda looked at both of them. "Maybe not. Help me reset the table and computer," she said.

"Why are you doing this?" Dr. Moon asked. Brenda switched on the computer, but nothing happened.

"The generator- I got it," Max said.

A few minutes later, the computer monitor lit up. "When I realized the hole was refilling itself, I threw the helmet camera down there," she said.

The three of them gathered around the monitor. There were fifteen seconds of footage before the sand covered the helmet cam. In those fifteen seconds, the helmet cam passed by what looked like the opening of two caves. Inside one of them, there was less than a second view of something which could be one of the beings. Max reached over, replayed the footage, freezing the image on the screen.

"Could this be one of them?" he asked.

Brenda tried zooming in on the image. "It could be, but let's pack up the equipment. I will take this back to New York, where I will be able to clean it up. Then we should know for sure," she said.

"And you will let me know as soon as you find out?" Max asked. Dr. Moon put his arm around Max's shoulder. "Indeed, we will," he said.

***

Max came up with an idea as he drove down Cactus Street toward his home in Spring Valley. When he was a student at Berkeley, he had met some guys he knew would jump at the chance to possibly discover something as phenomenal as this. From the footage he saw, and from his estimations, they shouldn't have to dig more than thirty or forty feet before reaching the first cave.

At the exact moments of Max's thoughts with Brenda beside him, Dr. Moon drove down Highway 395 toward Gillespie Field.

"It might have been a mistake to leave all that equipment with Max," Brenda said.

"Do you think he might try something stupid?" Dr. Moon asked.

"Yes, because he's smart. You and I have already thought of doing what I believe Max will attempt, and the only reason we didn't is because of what the male being told you," Brenda said.

"You may be right. I'll call Max as soon as we land in New York," Dr. Moon said.

Three days later, Maxwell Culverhouse stood inside the hole he and his two friends had dug. The rented backhoe would only reach ten feet. The rest would need to be dug by hand. His thoughts were on his last conversation with Dr. Moon. Max believed that Dr. Moon had been wrong when he said the beings would let them dig deep enough to reach the caves, but he was the one in the wrong. He watched in horror as his two friends disappeared under the sand. So did his thoughts of fame and social recognition when he realized his demise. Although his wits told him to run, one step later, his own head disappeared.

PRESENT DAY

Dr. Kenneth Moon thought of Max and the others who had tried to find the underworld. The trap had been set many times over, and many people had lost their lives. Now the time had come for him to return to his family. Brenda Carson would think him dead, and she would continue the quest to feed the beings.

IN SEARCH OF BECKA

CHAPTER 14

Max awoke to the sun shining on his face. The bedside clock read six forty-five a.m. "Not again," he thought as he jumped out of bed, ran into the bathroom, and turned on the shower. "Becka!" he yelled at the top of his voice. A few minutes later, his wife appeared at the door. "Why didn't you wake me? I told you if I was late for work one more time, they were going to fire me. You know if they do, we will lose this house," he yelled.

Becka walked up next to the shower, snatched back the curtain, then stomped her foot on the floor. "How in the world can you stand there and blame me? I woke you three times. Besides, I told you last night you shouldn't be drinking all that beer. So, this is your fault, A-hole!" she yelled.

"Alright, alright. Just go fix me something to eat," Max said.

"Yeah, right. You hold your breath on that happening, kiddo," Becka said as she walked out of the room, slamming the door behind her.

Max poured himself a cup of coffee. Becka was nowhere in sight. "I'm leaving now!" he yelled—still no reply from his wife. *Hell, this isn't the first time she's been angry. I'll buy her some flowers on my way home,* he thought as he slid behind his truck's steering wheel. He sat the coffee on the seat beside him, started the engine, and pulled out onto the highway. He looked at his gas gauge. He had enough to make it to his job, but thought *what the hell*? He was already late, and besides that, he was also hungry. He made up his mind that he would stop at the boy's store in Slap Out.

He felt the wet stain hit his leg before he felt the burning sensation from the coffee. "Dammit! Dammit! Dammit!" he said aloud as he reached for the glove box, hoping to find a napkin or something he could use to wipe up the spill. He didn't realize his foot had pushed down on the gas pedal. His truck moving at a speed of more than seventy miles per hour as it left the highway, slammed into an oak tree he did not see.

Max awoke to the soft kisses on the side of his face. He opened his eyes, coming face to face with the ugliest creature he had ever seen. "What the hell!!" he yelled. The big, black, and tan dog jumped away from him. Max sat up and looked around. He seemed to be sitting in a field of broom sage. Max stood up and was knee-deep in the tall grass. He saw a small path just wide enough to place one foot in front of the other. The big dog stood in the middle of the trail, looking up at him. "You're not going to bite me, are you, boy?" Max asked. The big dog shook his head from side to side. Max laughed at the dog's gesture. "Yeah, like you can understand me," he said. The big dog nodded his head. Again, Max laughed.

"Okay then, Mr. Smarty, can you tell me where I am?"

"You're in the middle of my owner's field," the dog said.

Max took several steps backward before he tripped and fell to the ground. The big dog walked over and looked down at him. Once again, Max stood to his feet. He turned in a complete circle.

"Who's out there?" he yelled. No one answered him.

"Look, whoever you are, this isn't funny. Now stand up and show yourself."

"I am standing up," the big dog said.

First, with his right hand, then with his left, Max slapped himself on the sides of his head. "Wake up, wake up! This can't be real. I need to wake up".

"Look, mister, from where I stand, it looks to me like you are as awake as you will ever be," the big dog said.

"Okay, let's just say for my own sanity, a black and tan hound dog can actually talk. I will ask you a question: Where am I, and how did I get here?"

"Well, mister, that's actually two questions, and the truth is, I can answer only one of them. I don't' know where you came from, and I have already told you that we are standing in the middle of my owner's hayfield."

"I need to go home."

"Where is your home?" asked the dog. Max looked down at him and shook his head, and said nothing. "You don't remember, do you?"

Again, Max shook his head. The big dog stuck out his left front paw. "My name is Old Blue. If you would like, I can help you find your way home, or at least introduce you to someone who can," he said. Once again, Max started laughing.

"Why are you laughing?" Old Blue asked.

"I don't mean no disrespect, but why would someone name you Old Blue when it's obvious you are black and tan?" Max said.

This time it was Old Blue who laughed. "That question, my new-found friend, you will need to ask the idiot who named me," he said.

"And just where can I find that idiot?" Max asked.

"Oh, he's not important. Right now, you need to follow this path. It will lead you to a farm. When you get there, ask for Becka. I believe she will be able to help you find your way home," stated Old Blue.

"Where are you going?" Max asked.

"Well, I was chasing me a rabbit when I came upon you. So, now, I'm going to try and pick up his scent again."

Max watched as Old Blue ran past him and disappeared into the tall grass. He had been walking for over an hour when he saw what he thought to be a large rock. As he got closer, he realized the rock had four legs and was waving them in the air as if it were swimming. "Hey, you, how about a little help here?" it said. Once again, Max laughed. He reached down and flipped the turtle over onto its belly. "Gee, thanks, mister. I was beginning to think no one would ever come along," the turtle said.

"How did you get yourself into that situation?" Max asked. "I was trying to do a triple somersault, and I missed the third run, mister. My name is Tom Tom, the Turtle, and I am practicing for the Olympics."

Once again, for sanity's sake, Max went along with this strange event.

"My name is Max, and I am on my way to find a woman by the name of Becka. Old Blue told me her farm was somewhere along this path. Do you know how much further it is?" he asked.

"Oh, yeah. It's not much further. I tell you what, if you carry me, I'll show you the way," Tom Tom said. Max reached down, picked up the turtle, and carried it with both hands. Two hours later, they came to the edge of a river. Max guessed it to be measured at least one hundred yards across. He was twenty-five years old and had quit smoking two years ago.

"I don't know if I can swim that far," he said.

"Oh, no. You don't have to swim. The river isn't very deep. You should be able to walk most of the way," Tom Tom the Turtle said.

Max stepped down into the river. It was like he was floating on air, except Max knew he was sinking into the water. Letting go of Tom Tom, Max fought his way back up to the surface. He saw the turtle's head rise above the water. "What the hell, Tom Tom! I thought you said it wasn't deep!" he yelled.

"Sorry, Max. My bad. Hey, don't you have a sense of humor? You go ahead and swim. I'm sure you can make it. Becka's farm is just over that hill. Tell her when you see her, old Tom Tom, the Turtle, said hi."

Max watched as the turtle's head went out of sight under the water. Climbing back onto the riverbank and realizing he had no other choice, he dove headfirst into the water. Swimming as far as he could, Max rolled over onto his back and allowed himself to float. As soon as he caught his breath, he swam the remaining yardage to the shore. Max climbed out of the water and rested on the river's embankment of grass. Placing his hand on his chest, he noticed it was moving up and down at a fast pace, and he could hear his heartbeat. He tried to think of how he had gotten himself into this strange situation, but all Max could remember was his own name.

"Where are you going?" someone asked. Max rolled to his side. He found himself face to face with a gray squirrel. *Oh, shit. Not again?* he thought. "Can't you speak? I asked you where you were going?" the squirrel said.

"I'm looking for Becka," Max said.

"Oh! Well, my friend, I hate to tell you this, but you are on the wrong side of the river. Becka's farm is over there two miles to the north," the squirrel said.

"But Tom Tom told me Becka's farm was just over this hill."

"Oh, no, no, no. You didn't listen to him. Let me tell you about Tom Tom. For starters, you shouldn't have believed a single word he said—that lying turtle. I'll bet when you met him, he was lying on his back. Old Blue did that to him, but he would have returned later and flipped him back over. You see, one time Tom Tom told Old Blue he knew where a family of rabbits lived. Not that Old Blue would have hurt any of those rabbits, he just liked chasing them through the tall grass. Anyway, that lying turtle only wanted Old Blue to carry him back here to this river. Now, I'm going to go out on a limb here, no pun intended, and say you carried Tom Tom down here to the river, right?" the squirrel said.

Max stood to his feet, looking back across the river. "Do you have a name?" he asked, without looking down at the squirrel.

"Yeah, it's Billy, but everyone just calls me Squirrel. It's always, 'hey Squirrel this,' or 'hey Squirrel that'. 'Squirrel will you go here, 'Squirrel, will you go there?' No one, and I mean no one, ever calls me by my name except for maybe my Momma and Papa, and maybe my sixteen brothers, and my ten sisters, and maybe my eight uncles." said the squirrel.

"Okay, okay. I get it. So, you are telling me Becka's farm is across the river, to the north?" Max asked.

"Yeah, yeah, yeah, but from the looks of that hole in your head, I don't think you would be able to make it back across. Why don't you lay down and rest? I'll go find Walley. He will help you get across," Billy said.

"Who's Walley?" Max asked.

"Walley is a friend. You can trust him and Max, if you see that lying turtle, just flip him over onto his back; sooner or later, someone will come along and right him."

Max sat down on the grass. He watched the squirrel run along the river bank until it was out of sight. Reaching up, touching his head, not feeling the hole that Billy spoke about, Max lay down on his back and closed his eyes.

"Hey buddy, Max, is that you?" Max sat up and looked around but didn't see anyone. When he stood to his feet and looked down into the river, he took several steps back. "You must be Walley," he said.

"No, my name is Crock. Walley had to go visit a sick friend, so he sent me," he said.

"But, you're an alligator," Max said.

"I know, I know. But, let's not go there, okay? I'm here to help you cross the river," Crock said.

"What do you want me to do? Get on your back?" Max asked.

"Hell, no. I ain't no horse. Just hold on to the end of my tail, and I will float you across," Crock said.

Once again, Max dove headfirst into the water. True to his word, Crock pulled him across the river.

"Hey, Max. You need to wait here. Becka said she would come to find you herself. Now, be sure you stay in this exact spot." Before Max could thank him, Crock's head disappeared under the water. He lay down on the ground and closed his eyes.

***

Becka rushed through the doors to the emergency room at City Memorial Hospital near Slap Out, Alabama. She literally ran up to the desk.

"My name is Becka Hinton. My husband, Max, was brought here by ambulance. Can you tell me where he is?" she asked. The nurse behind the desk punched in the name Max Hinton on her computer.

"Yes, he is on the third floor. They are taking him into surgery as we speak," she said. "Surgery? What kind of surgery?" Becka asked.

"It doesn't say, but if you go up to the third floor, you will see a desk as soon as you step off the elevator. Someone there will be able to help you," the nurse said.

When the elevator door opened, Becka was relieved to see a familiar face. Max's best friend, Walley, stood in the waiting area. She walked up to him.

"How is he?" she asked.

"It's still too early to tell. He banged his head. They said his brain might swell, so they're going to drill a hole in his skull."

Becka reached out and grabbed Walley's arm. "Please, tell me he will be okay," she said. Walley placed both hands on her shoulders, then kissed her forehead.

"Sure he will," he said. The two of them sat in the waiting area, watching a set of doors that lead to the operating rooms. A half-hour went by before the doctor came through them. Both Becka and Walley stood and walked to meet him. Becka felt relieved when she saw the smile come across the doctor's face.

"How is he?" she asked. The doctor touched her arm.

"Come, let's have a seat," he said. All three sat on a couch with the doctor in the middle. "Right now, he is stable. We have relieved the pressure from his brain. We are going to keep him in a coma until all the swelling dissipates," the doctor said.

"How long?" Walley asked.

"Two days, maybe three. We don't know yet, but the good news is that we have placed electrodes on his head. This tells us right now he does have a sizable amount of brain activity," the doctor said.

"How is this good news?" Becka asked. The doctor's pager beeped. He pulled it out of his pocket and looked at it before he stood.

"I'm sorry. I have to go. But, to answer your question, as long as he has this much brain activity, it means he is fighting hard for his life."

"Can we go see him?" Becka asked.

"It shouldn't be a problem. They should be putting him in a room now. Check with the nurse. She will let you know where he is and when you may see him." Both Becka and Walley thanked the doctor before walking over to the desk.

***

Max awoke to the sound of what he believed to be a woman screaming in his ear. Instead, he found himself face to face with a mountain lion. Her mouth was wide open as the drool dripped from her long sharp teeth. Max sat up. He saw the lion raise its paw. He was able to turn to his side as the big paw came toward him. Her long, sharp claw hit his shoulder, ripping a six-inch gash down his arm. He did the only thing he could think of... he wrapped both arms around the lion, then rolled over and over on the ground until he splashed down into the river. He swam away from the shore before turning to see if the lion had followed him. To his surprise and relief, she was nowhere in sight. He kicked his feet and waved his arms, trying to stay afloat. He realized he was bleeding. He swam back to the shore, then crawled up onto the bank. Wanting to flee, but not knowing which direction the angry lion had traveled, he pulled his shirt over his head and wrapped it around the cut on his arm. He seemed to be falling in and out of consciousness.

"Max, wake up. We need to go before she comes back. Max, please wake up."

The female voice seemed real. Max opened his eyes, and a snow-white horse stood beside him. "Good, you are awake. Now, grab my leg and pull yourself up. Then climb onto my back." Max felt himself moving in slow motion but did as she said. He held onto her long, white mane as she ran through the tall grass. When she came to a stop, Max felt himself falling through the air. He felt his breath leave his body from the impact with the ground. He closed his eyes, trying to block out the pain. "You are safe now. All you have to do is breathe. You will be home soon," the white horse said.

***

Three days after the accident, Max opened his eyes. He lay in the middle of a bed with the covers pulled up around his neck. A familiar face looked down at him with tear-stained eyes. "Welcome back," Becka said.

Max smiled at his wife and said, "I've been searching for you."

ABOUT THE AUTHOR

James F. Causey born and raised in Alabama is a father, an avid reader, and an inspired writer who enjoys creatively writing new adventures to entertain the mind. Causation is book one in the series of the Chronicles of James.